Prayer Warriors
A Near-Future Tale

by
James J. Stewart

ISBN: 978-0-9861334-8-0

To My Dad, Frank W. Stewart (1910-1996):

*His wisdom and joy continue
to inspire and energize me.*

1.
Sadness on the Sea

Andy Hickman's hair rustled slightly in the Caribbean Sea's breeze. Just over six feet tall, he was slender and clean-shaven, and his features were angular and well proportioned. His eyes, distinctively mallard-green, were steady though sad. His wife, Abby, said he had bedroom eyes, but today those eyes had tears. Quite muscular, Andy moved with a casual but erect posture.

Standing on the fantail of the sailing ship, *Polynesia*, he looked down at the brass label on the burial urn: "Andrew Tobias Hickman - 1930-2036." Andy slowly turned the urn, as if he could find some reason for his father's ashes not to be inside. "Mom, don't you want to do the honors of scattering Dad's ashes?"

His mother, Trina, shook her head. Despite her years, she was still trim, petite, blonde, and blue-eyed. "No, son, it is going to be hard enough for me to stand here and watch you do it." She turned to the two others who were standing there. "Mike, Debbie, I really appreciate you being here for this. You met Huck a couple of years before I did."

Mike was quite dark, with Hispanic skin stretched tightly over his expressive face. His deep-set eyes were almost black, and his matching hair was combed straight back. He nodded. "We were fresh out of college and newlyweds. He sensed we were struggling to cope with a lot of things, and he took us under his wing."

Debbie, Mike's wife, wiped away a tear and tried to smile. "With Huck's help, we were just beginning to get our act together when you came along. She was stunningly attractive, with homegrown long black lashes surrounding eyes that had the color of pure caramel. "How old was Huck when you two got married?"

Trina wiped her tears with a handkerchief. "Huck was seventy, and I was twenty-two. Everyone said I was a fool for asking him to marry me, but God had set us up."

Andy looked up from the urn. "Tell them the story, Mom, unless you've already told them."

Trina shook her head. "The only people in the world I've told have been you, Linda, and Bill. You listened and understood, Andy, but your sister and brother shook their heads in disbelief."

"Tell us," said Debbie and Mike, almost at once.

Trina nodded. "Okay." For a moment, she glanced out over the water. "Just after Huck retired, he was in his apartment alone on New Year's Eve, and after midnight, he decided to read the Bible before going to bed. For some reason, he turned to Genesis 24, read the whole chapter about Abraham sending his servant to secure a wife for his son, Isaac. Then Huck started talking to God aloud. He talked to God about the three women he had known and fallen in love with - not at the same time, of course. He also pointed out to God that, despite his best efforts, he had not gotten married. Then he talked about Abraham's servant, who made a bargain with God in a prayer, and God had answered that prayer, resulting in Rebecca's going with the servant to be wed to Isaac.

"Huck once told me it was one of the few times throughout his life that he yelled at God. That story made getting a wife look so easy, he told God. Next, Huck came up with a question that he could ask almost anyone. He told God that if God wanted him to be married, he would ask a woman a particular question about her faith, she would say yes, and afterward she would ask him to marry her."

Debbie's eyes grew wide. "That's incredible! Is that what happened?"

Trina nodded. "When I was home on my winter break the December of my senior year at the University of Texas, I had a vivid dream in which a man whose face I could not see in the dream asked me a question about my faith, I said yes, and then I asked him to marry me. In the dream, it seemed completely natural. I awakened believing that the dream was prophetic. I knew it was going to happen for me. The following spring, my parents asked Huck to come over for dinner, to get to know him. I was home from college, having just graduated, and I met Huck for the first time that evening at dinner. As we were eating dessert, Huck asked me the question I had heard in the dream. I swallowed and said yes, and then without hesitation I asked Huck to marry me. He said, 'Absolutely!' You should have seen my parents' faces!"

Mike's mouth hung open, and then he closed it a moment. "That actually happened?"

Trina nodded.

Debbie laughed. "Then what happened?"

"Huck told my parents and me about his conversation with God five years earlier. Then I told Huck and my parents about the dream I had had the previous December. After we finished our dessert, we prayed about it together. My Dad read Genesis 24 aloud to all of us, and then we talked about what friends and family were going to say. Most of Huck's family had already gone home to heaven except for a few cousins, along with two nieces and a nephew."

Mike nodded. "So what did you and Huck do?"

"Huck's roommate from his seminary days had a church about six hundred miles north of there. The next day we drove up there, and that evening Huck and I were married."

Andy nodded. "I was born about ten months later, right?"

Trina nodded her head. "After you were born, we went through three miscarriages before I got pregnant with Linda. I was still nursing Linda when I got pregnant with Bill. At the time of our wedding, many people told us that they thought our marriage wouldn't last more than a month, or at most a year." She paused to wipe away another tear. "Two months ago, Huck and I celebrated thirty-five years together – ours was a millennial marriage, with the wedding being in the spring of 2000. Andy, Huck was so excited when you and Abby gave us our first grandson." She paused to look directly at Andy. "I wish Abby, Linda, and Bill could be here with us."

"I know, Mom, but as you know, Abby is almost eight months along with our second pregnancy, and Linda is still taking care of Bill after that collision he had a month ago. A tear rolled down Andy's cheek, and he looked at the urn again. "I guess its time to do this, isn't it?"

The others nodded. Andy took the lid off the urn and slowly poured the ashes into the ocean. He put the lid back on, and then he offered it to his Mom. "Do you want to keep it?"

She shook her head. "No, do you?"

For just a moment, he stared at the urn again, and then he hurled it into the ocean.

Since it was almost time for dinner, they headed toward the dining area. Mike asked, "Andy, I know that you and your Dad have the same name. Does your birth certificate include junior?"

Andy shook his head as they started down the gangway. "No. Actually, my certificate indicates that I am the eighth man with my name. My oldest is the ninth, but we're calling him Toby, as you know. The only time I ever use my full legal name is on rare occasions for legal documents. Toby will probably do the same, as Dad did."

In the dining area, the four of them took a corner table. After they placed their orders, Trina looked at her son and touched his arm. "Andy, do you think you have inherited the gift from your Dad? You've never said anything about it."

He shook his head. "I honestly don't know that it is a gift, Mom. He gave me many lessons in how to pray. With me, he never referred to it as being a gift. At the beginning, he told me that he wanted to teach me how to be a prayer warrior, just as his father had taught him, going back for many generations."

Andy looked at Mike and Debbie. "If you've not heard that term before, to be a prayer warrior means to engage in a spiritual battle, fighting the good fight of faith. Dad taught me the importance of wearing the full armor of God as described in the book of Ephesians while fighting spiritual battles."

He turned back to his Mom. "Dad told me that sometimes he felt the warmth and power of the Holy Spirit when he prayed during hospital calls or on pastoral calls in people's homes. Is that what you're talking about, Mom?"

Trina nodded. "I experienced that gift - and I have always thought of it as a gift - a few times when we prayed for someone together. I've consistently thought of it as a gift because those who were healed sometimes spoke of it as such."

Debbie touched Trina's arm. "What gift?"

Trina turned to her with a small smile. "I guess many would call it a spiritual gift. There are lists of spiritual gifts found in Romans 12, 1 Corinthians 12, and Ephesians 4."

Trina paused, thoughtful. "Until now, it has not been discussed outside of our immediate family. At this moment, you and Mike are hearing it mentioned for the first time, and I'd appreciate it very much if you kept it to yourselves."

"What are you talking about?" asked Mike.

Trina was quiet a moment. "You and Debbie finally joined our church family shortly after Huck and I got married. A number of times both of you have mentioned how Huck prayed. Although Huck was almost casual when he was praying, it was also reverential, humble, and intimate. He considered Jesus not merely his Savior but also his best friend and constant companion."

Debbie nodded. "Yes! He could pray long prayers that did not seem long at all. As we listened, it was as though we were joining Huck in another world. I gather that those public prayers were very different from his private prayers on behalf of those who were sick, injured, having other serious difficulties."

Mike nodded. "I'm not surprised. After the two of you prayed for our friend, Steve Lyman, he told me that I might call him crazy, but as the warmth flowed through him, he knew that he would be out of the hospital soon.

He was."

Trina smiled. "When Huck prayed for someone's healing or deliverance, most of the prayer was silent. He would pray a sort of opening declaration to God, and then he would pray silently until he simply said, 'Amen,'"

Andy nodded. "Since I'm not a pastor, I don't have occasions to pray over people the way Dad did."

As they ate, they told other stories of their experiences with Huck. Mike enjoyed talking about Huck almost as much as Andy and Trina did. "One Sunday after his communion prayer, Huck invited us to look into the cup in our hand as we waited for everyone to be served. That particular Sunday, Debbie and I were sitting further towards the front than usual, and I could see one of the lights above us reflected from the surface of the grape juice. My own pulse was making the light's reflection quiver. For just a moment, I imagined the beating of our Lord's heart as He died upon the cross. I'll never forget that moment."

Debbie smiled. "When Huck baptized us, I insisted on Mike going first. Then when I was baptized, when I came up out of the water Huck was praying loudly, and Mike was grinning. I had forgotten to wear anything under the baptismal robe, and it clung to my skin."

Mike laughed. "Huck saved her from embarrassment by loudly saying 'Let us pray,' and starting his prayer while she was still under the water, and everyone bowed their heads!"

After dessert, they went to the top deck, where passengers could enjoy the clear night and twinkling stars. They continued telling stories until well after midnight.

When the others went back to their cabins, Andy went to the bow of the *Polynesia*. For nearly an hour, he stood there thinking about his Dad, while the warm Virgin Islands wind whipped his hair. Glancing upward to the stars and a half-full moon, he murmured, "Dad, I know your touch sometimes brought healing, and you taught me how to be a prayer warrior, but do I have some kind of spiritual gift like the way Mom talks about it? Ask Jesus, will you? If I have such a gift, I would like to know. Abby knows that, for generations, the first born in the Hickman family has been taught how to be a prayer warrior. She and I have not considered my having some kind of spiritual gift. If I do, I'm not sure I'm ready to use it." He continued to stare at the stars until well after midnight.

He did not hear anyone approaching him before fingers touched his elbow. He looked down into the eyes of a petite woman in a cutoff T-shirt and shorts. "Would you like some company?" she asked.

"Hi." He paused. "I guess so. I scattered my Dad's ashes over the water earlier, and I was kind of talking to him. Company's welcome though."

"Are you sure?"

"Yeah. I'm Andy. You?"

"I'm Kristal. You don't look like you're forty yet, so your Dad must have been young when he died."

Andy shook his head and smiled. "Not really. When I was born, he was seventy-one. Two months ago, he and my Mom celebrated their thirty-fifth anniversary."

Her eyes grew wide. "What? Was that your Mom with you on the stern? She ... I don't know what to say!"

Andy decided to make the story sound colorful. "When she asked him to marry her in front of her folks, he was seventy, and she was twenty-two."

"Holy ...."

"That's kind of close! My Dad was a pastor for five

decades before he retired. He died two months short of his 106th birthday."

"He was born in 1930?"

"Right, and this being 2036, he hadn't yet celebrated his birthday this year."

"Wow!" She paused. "Are you married?"

"Yes, I'm married to a beautiful woman who is eight months along with our second child. My wife and I gave my Dad and Mom their first grandson nearly two years ago. She's not here with me to say good-bye to my Dad because the doctor wouldn't allow it." He turned towards her to face her directly. "Are you on this cruise with family?"

She nodded. "I'm traveling with my two brothers and a sister. You said your Dad was a pastor. Are you a pastor too?"

"No, I'm a hospital administrator."

"Oh." She looked down. "If you were a pastor like your Dad, I'd ask you to pray for me."

"I can pray for you. It's not astrophysics. What would you like me to talk to God about?"

"I'm thirty, and it looks like I might not reach thirty-one. I've got terminal cancer."

"Do you want me to pray aloud or silently?"

"Silently will be okay, I guess."

"Okay, I'll put my hand on top of your head while I pray, all right?"

"Okay."

A few minutes later, Andy lifted his hand, and he said, "Amen."

Kristal sat down on a cushioned bench nearby. "Thank you. I feel like I'm at peace for the first time in weeks." Andy also sat down. They sat there in silence for several minutes, and then she stood up. "Do you think your wife would mind if I gave you a hug?"

Andy smiled and stood up. "Okay."

Kristal hugged him hard, and then she stepped back. "I'm going to my cabin and pray some more. I'll see you tomorrow, I hope. Thank you, thank you again, Andy."

He nodded. "You're welcome, Kristal."

+ + +

In her cabin, Trina felt tired and was already in bed. Turning onto her stomach, she raised herself up so that she was on her knees, with her forehead on her pillow. She prayed softly. "Father, I didn't feel entirely comfortable at first, sharing so much with Mike and Debbie, but I know we can trust them. You know, Lord, that there was so much I could have told others but never will. You know that when I married Huck, I was scared to death. I knew within my heart that marrying Huck was right, but at first, I didn't even find him attractive. It took months for me to learn to love him. Now, there's this big gaping hole inside me that nothing can fill but you."

Trina turned on her side. "Andy seems to be just like Huck in this respect, Lord. He seems to agree with Huck's insistence that it not be called a gift." Turning off the light by her bed, she paused to shift and get more comfortable. "None of us alive on this Earth could ever do much good without your mercy and grace. I've seen how nothing is too difficult for you. You seem to be nudging me into believing that Mike is facing some kind of sickness. I lift him up to you and your mercy, Lord. Mike is so blessed to have Debbie. She is amazingly beautiful inside and out. I have no doubt that you are using Mike for Debbie and vice versa. Please strengthen their marriage."

Trina fluffed her pillow. "I know that Abby is going to have another boy, Lord, and knowing Andy, I'm sure he loves that. Andy and Huck were so close. I'm sure he aches inside like I do. It will be no surprise, Lord, if you use Andy as powerfully as you used Huck, only I think you'll use him in some different ways, won't you, Lord?" She took a deep breath and sighed. "I wish Linda and Bill could have been here today, Lord. Please bless them...." She drifted off to sleep.

2.
Return to Routine

The return flight from the Virgin Islands touched down in Los Angeles on Saturday afternoon, and Mike and Debbie dropped him off at home just in time to have dinner with Abby and little Toby. His son was sound asleep in his crib as he and Abby embraced.

Andy looked down at his very pregnant and voluptuous Abby. "The last time a woman hugged me, it was aboard the *Polynesia*. It was the last night of the cruise. She has cancer, and she asked me to pray for her. It was a hug of gratitude."

Seven inches shorter than Andy, Abby looked up at him, radiant and happy. "Was she as preggers as I am?"

He laughed. "Not at all!"

"What's her name?"

"Kristal."

"Let's pray for her this evening."

He nodded. They enjoyed the rest of the evening, and they watched an old movie together until it was late. Just before turning off the lights for the night, they prayed for their children, the church, and Kristal.

The next day, Andy had severe jet lag. Most of the morning they were at church, and he was in a fog. Absentmindedly, he heard Trina complement their pastor on his sermon, and he thought of his Dad. After church, they stopped at a drive-through and got some hamburgers. Andy and Abby took Toby to a park, and he nursed from a bottle, while his parents ate their burgers and fries. Back at their home that afternoon, Andy took a long nap, and Abby chatted with her parents over the phone.

Monday, Andy's jet lag seemed to have subsided somewhat. In his office at Seaside Hospital in Long Beach, Andy leaned back in his chair and stared out his one-way-glass window. At the end of the street, he could see a tiny piece of the ocean. He turned back to his desk and pulled up the admissions list on his monitor. He touched a button. "Janet?"

A soprano voice answered, "Yes, sir?"

"I don't have any appointments this morning, do I?"

"No. You have a Chamber of Commerce luncheon in our cafeteria at 12:30, and you're meeting with the Mayor here in your office at 3:00. You've got nothing pressing this morning."

"Thanks. I see two names on the admissions list that I recognize. Page me if I'm needed."

"Okay."

Andy stood up, buttoned his suit coat, and headed out to the elevators. The original Seaside Hospital was now a park on Fourteenth Street. This hospital was quite different from the first. It had been a hotel for decades, which was converted to condominiums. Six years previously, an earthquake severely damaged that historic structure. A granddaughter of Henry Kaiser, the billionaire shipbuilder and health plan founder, paid a good price to each of the condominium homeowners, and built this hospital on the site. It had been controversial because it was a little taller than the previous complex. The result of the redevelopment was five floors of patient rooms above the ground floor. There were three more floors below ground with surgery suites, labs, and physicians' offices surrounding an open atrium reaching the second floor.

One of the first things Andy did as administrator was to develop the hospital's flat roof into a fully landscaped park with picnic tables. He had been negotiating for property north of the hospital for a parking garage, but that had fallen through. Meanwhile, city buses and taxicabs did a brisk business to and from the hospital, and a shuttle transported the staff to and from off-site reserved parking.

Getting on the elevator, Andy pushed the "5," and moments later, he was striding down the hallway. At room 5014, he knocked. A woman's voice inside said to come in. As Andy approached the bed, the woman asked, are you Dr. Cochran?" The slender woman on the bed had the head of the bed raised, and cascades of dark blonde hair flowed over her shoulders.

"No," Andy replied, "I'm the hospital administrator. I'm sure you don't recognize me. It's been more than twenty years since you and I have seen each other. I'm Andy Hickman."

Her mouth opened slightly, as her eyes grew wider. "Andy? Andy Hickman? Did you go to Bancroft Junior High?"

"Guilty! I had a huge crush on you, Rita, in the seventh grade. When I finally came around to ask you out, you were already going steady with Paul Barger and turned me down."

She nodded. "Paul was killed by an IUD in Afghanistan. How long have you been here at Seaside?"

"I was hired before it opened. Let me use your phone a moment." He picked up the receiver and punched a number. "Hey, John, this is Andy."

"Good morning, Andy. What's up?"

"I walked into 5014 a few minutes ago, and Rita

14

McLaughlin thought I was you. If you're going to be here soon, I'll wait for you. I've got something to discuss with you after you see your patient."

"I take it she's an old friend?"

Andy smiled. "Since junior high school."

"I'm getting out of my scrubs and should be there pretty quickly."

"Good. I'll stick around a few minutes. See ya." Andy put the receiver back. "Dr. Cochran will be here in less than five minutes I would imagine. He was in surgery until a minute or so ago." He paused. "Is there anything I can do for you, Rita?"

"Yeah. I know you're a Christian because your Dad was a pastor. Would you pray for me?"

"Sure. May I put my hand on your shoulder while I pray?"

"Sure."

He closed his eyes and was silent for about a minute. "Thank you for hearing my prayer for Rita, Lord. I surrender her to you in Jesus' name. Amen." There was a knock on the door. "Hey, John, good morning again. I'll be out at the nurses' station when you're done here."

"Good morning."

Andy looked down at Rita. "It's been good to see you again, Rita. I'm married to Abby Smith, and I'll tell her I saw you."

"Terrific! Tell Abby hello for me. Do you two have any kids?"

He nodded. "A boy, two, and one on the way that's due within a month. I'll let you talk to Dr. Cochran now." He smiled, turned, and went outside.

The doctor closed the door. More than six feet six inches tall, he towered over his patient, but his deep bass voice was soft and comforting. "Miss McLaughlin,

15

your test results do not look encouraging. You knew already that you have tumors in both your breasts, but it appears that the cancer may already have spread. If it has, you're facing the possibility of both a more extensive surgery and chemotherapy."

Rita nodded. "I understand. Do you still have me scheduled for first thing tomorrow morning?"

The surgeon nodded. "Your final prep will begin around seven, and you'll be under anesthesia by eight."

"I want the mammograms repeated."

He shook his head. "It's not necessary. There's no doubt that you have cancer."

"I trust your judgment as a surgeon, Dr. Cochran, but I still want tests to confirm the location of the cancer."

"If your insurance refuses to cover the cost, you'll have to pay for the tests."

"I understand. I won't sign off the permission for surgery until the cancer is confirmed once more."

"Did Andy, suggest this to you?"

She shook her head. "Andy did not even ask me why I was here. We talked about our days at Bancroft Junior High, and then I asked him to pray for me. I saw you standing outside the door while he was praying."

John nodded. "Okay. I'll order the tests. We'll get them done this afternoon. If the tests reveal anything new, I'll see you again this evening. Otherwise, I'll see you tomorrow morning, okay?"

"Thank you."

"You're welcome. Your anesthesiologist will be here in a little while to talk to you about her part in all of this. Her name is Dr. Prudy Skivins, okay?"

"Okay. I'll see you later."

He nodded, turned, and left. Outside, at the nurses'

station, he saw Andy chatting with one of them. He looked up and beckoned him towards the conference room.

As he closed the door, Andy said, "While you were in surgery, John, the da Vinci Surgical System robotic unit you ordered arrived."

"Excellent! It got here sooner than we expected."

They sat down at the conference table. Andy looked at his friend. "Did you order everything that is going to be needed in support of that equipment, or did you hold off on anything?"

John shook his head. "No, I ordered everything the sales rep recommended. I can test it out this evening and make sure everything is in order. On another subject, I guess you've known Miss McLaughlin for a long time."

"Not really. This is the first time I've seen her in more than twenty years. As per policy, I did not ask her why she is here. She simply asked me to pray for her, which I was more than willing to do. Did that bother you?"

"No, but she asked to have her tests repeated, and I asked her if you had suggested it. She assured me the answer was no, and I believed her. It's not a problem, Andy. I know you to be an ethical man."

Andy nodded. "Good. I have another old friend, Ken Kaiser, down on the first floor. I don't think he's your patient, is he?"

"No, I don't recognize the name."

"Okay." They stood up. "I may stop and check on Rita tomorrow or the next day simply because she's an old school friend."

"Okay." They headed out the door. As John headed towards the nurses' station, Andy headed for the elevators and pushed the down button.

On the first floor, as Andy approached room 1121, he could see Ken Kaiser. He was skinny as a rail and more than ten years younger, with brown hair and hazel eyes. Ken was sitting on the chair near his bed. Andy walked on in. "Hi, Ken!"

"Andy!" He stood up to shake Andy's hand. "It's great to see you. I was wondering if I might see you while I am here. I'm just getting cataracts in my left eye taken care of. Are you still trying to find land to build a parking garage for the hospital?"

Andy nodded. "Every time I think I've made progress, things crumble. That's life, I guess." He smiled.

Ken cocked his head to one side. "Do you remember the place where we set up the haunted house every Halloween when we were in high school?"

"Do you mean the old Cooper place?"

"Yeah, the city has wanted to do something about that eyesore for years, and then Dandy Cooper died. His will has been in probate for a couple of months now. While you were down in the Caribbean, someone called the police to report a bad odor coming from the house. That lead to inspections, and the house was condemned. When we were in school, you and I wondered why no houses had been built on the lots north and south of the Cooper place."

"Right! When Mr. Cooper let us set up the haunted house stuff, we had lots of space to set up scary stuff for the kids approaching the house."

Ken nodded. "As it turns out, that land was all part of the Cooper property. Dandy Cooper was a real eccentric who wanted to keep neighbors at a distance."

Andy's eyes grew wide, and he looked up at the ceiling. "Thanks, Lord!" He looked at Ken. "This means

18

that's easily enough land for a parking garage. I'll get on it as soon as I'm back in the office. If you're just getting Dr. Mounce to take out your cataracts, this is outpatient surgery, right?"

"Right. The next time you see me, I'll probably have a patch over my eye at church."

Andy smiled. "Right, so I'll see you Sunday, my friend."

"Okay." They shook hands, and Ken smiled as Andy left.

As he went out the door, Andy turned toward his office. He looked at his watch and smiled. There was just enough time to contact Greg Hosmar about the Cooper property before the Chamber of Commerce luncheon. He walked briskly past the elevators. As he entered his outer office, he spoke to Janet, his secretary. In her early fifties, she was always poised and dignified, and Andy had grown very fond of her. "Get Greg Hosmar on the phone. If he's not available, try to track him down. We may have a chance at some property for a parking lot that I did not consider. I've got to move fast."

She picked up her phone. "Okay."

Andy went into his office and closed the door. He closed his eyes and prayed silently, and then he sat down at his desk just as the phone rang. He picked up the receiver. "Yes?"

"I've got Greg Hosmar on the line."

"Thanks, Janet." She clicked off. "Greg! I'm glad I've caught you. Do you know anything about the property owned by the late Dandy Cooper?"

"That old house? Why are you interested in it?"

"I just learned that Mr. Cooper never had neighbors on either side of him because he owned those lots too.

Those three lots together might be enough for a parking garage. What do you think?"

"Wow! You may be right. That property is only a short distance from the hospital too. I'll get on this right now. If the overall size of the property is enough, we'll have to get a zoning variance from the City Council, but that should not be a problem. Tom Elliott, the architect for a couple of other parking garages in the area, is a friend of mine. I'll have him take a look at the situation."

"Okay, Greg. I have a Chamber of Commerce luncheon to go to in less than a half hour. Are you going to be there?"

"Not with this Cooper property situation. That's my focus until I get some answers."

"Good, keep me posted. I'm going to get going."

"Right, see you later." The connection ended.

+ + +

The following Tuesday morning, Andy met with Greg Hosmar and Tom Elliott in his office. The realtor was on the short side and had a slight stoop in his shoulders. He had many repeat customers, though certainly not from his appearance. His face might have been average looking except that his nose was much too big. Making up for his nose, he had a smile that would light up a room.

The other man was totally different. If you walked into a room full of people, you would never guess that Tom Elliott was an architect. When he needed to, he could look like a movie star at a premier, but most of the time his dress was strictly and deceptively blue-collar. He had eidetic memory, remembering perfectly every face or blueprint he had ever seen, remembering every conversation he had perpetually, as well as remembering every word of every book he had read.

After greeting the two men, Andy quickly got down to business. "Tom, tell me, is that property big enough for a multilevel parking garage?"

Tom Elliott smiled and nodded. "There's a property line variance on the back side of the properties that was originally set aside for an alley, and if you purchase the properties you get that extra twenty-two feet as well. That helps us immensely. Down at the Zoning Department I ran into another thing that adds an advantageous additional expense."

Andy looked at him skeptically. "How is an additional expense advantageous?"

"When I told them you were thinking about putting a multilevel parking garage on the site, they told me that we would have to put down some significant pilings to under-gird the foundation. You might think that's bad until you hear the reason that pilings are necessary. When the hospital was built, the contractor ran into a surprise when digging for the multilevel basement, isn't that right?"

Andy nodded. "Yes. There was a branch of an old flood-control conduit that the city records didn't show."

Tom smiled. "That same conduit runs under the old Cooper estate. If we build a parking garage on the surface without the pilings, eventually that conduit would collapse from the weight."

Greg Hosmar nodded. "Okay, so I can see why the pilings are necessary, but what's the advantage?"

Tom smiled. "I'm a history buff. I've loved our city's history ever since I went to Lakewood High School. When the city had no record of the flood-control conduit that was discovered during the hospital's construction, I went into the Press-Telegram morgue to do some research. On some microfiche copies of newspapers

21

from the 1930s, I found articles about Civil Conservation Corps projects launched within the city. That flood control project was never completed because the Japanese attacked Pearl Harbor. Anyway, the conduit is twelve feet wide and ten feet tall. If we can finance it, that conduit can be a tunnel that connects the parking garage with the hospital."

Andy whistled. "Praise God! This is an answer to prayer. With God's help, we'll get the financing. How much parking can we put there on the Cooper property?"

The architect was thoughtful. "With using those pilings along with earthquake construction standards, we'll have to do some surveys of the neighborhood, but I think you can get away with the same number of stories as that of the hospital. All three lots are old and wide. We can also go downward to the level of the proposed tunnel. I think we can build more than enough of what the hospital needs currently."

Andy's cell phone rang, and he looked at it. "Excuse me. It's my wife." He touched the phone's screen. "Hi, honey, what's up?"

Abby's voice was tense. "It's probably a false alarm, but I'm having labor pains. Paramedics are on their way. Dr. Fagin wants me to check into emergency, so I'll be there in less than ten minutes."

Andy stared into space, nodding. "Okay. I'll be waiting for you. I love you."

"I love you too." The connection ended, and he put the phone away.

"Evidently, my wife is having false labor pains. This is too soon. She's not due for a few more weeks. I'm going to meet her when she arrives at emergency." He paused. "This has been a memorable meeting, guys, but we've got to end it. Keep me posted, both of you." He started toward the door.

Tom got up. "I'll draw up some preliminary plans while Greg does the realty work."

Greg also stood up. "Right. We'll see you later, Andy."

Andy nodded. "Right. Later, guys." He left, and the other men followed him.

+ + +

At her home, Trina was gazing into her freezer when the doorbell rang. Taking out a package of chicken thighs and placing them on the sink counter, she dried her hands on her apron and went to the front door. After glancing at the security monitor in the corner, she flung open the door. "Hey, kids, this is a nice surprise!" She opened the screen door. "Come in! Come in!"

Linda, her daughter, greeted Trina with a hug. "We just had to come over and have you tell us about the cruise!"

Bill, Trina's son, followed his sister in on crutches. "Yeah! We want to hear all about it! After that, I've got some news for you."

"News?"

"Later, Mom, I'll tell you after you tell us about the cruise."

"Okay, come on in and sit down. I'm sure you want to get off of those crutches. Your wreck was what, six weeks ago? How much longer will you need them?"

"Probably another week or two"

As they gathered in the living room, Trina told them about scattering the ashes, and later she told them about the stories they swapped about Huck. And then she paused. "Okay, Bill, what's your news?"

"I think Linda should tell you her news first."

"You have news, too, Linda?"

"Well, okay, but … okay, Sam and I have set a date, and we've set the date with Pastor Paul."

"Great! It's about time! You two have been engaged for, what, two years?"

"Twenty-two months, two weeks, and three days." They all laughed.

"Okay, Bill, now it's your turn."

He nodded. "Brooke brought a lemon sponge cake over to me last evening, and I asked her to marry me."

"Wonderful!" Trina smiled broadly for the first time since Huck died. "Did you give her a ring?"

"Of course, Mom, and today she is showing it to all of her friends. She'll be coming over in a little while, and Sam will too. It's my treat to take us all out to dinner tonight."

"Fantastic!" Trina continued smiling.

"As you know, Brooke's folks died in a collision with a drunk driver's car two years ago, so I've told her that I'll cover the cost of a small wedding in the church before we honeymoon in New Zealand. I've already bought the tickets for us to leave the last weekend of next month."

"Great! Be sure to call Andy and Abby."

"I will."

3.
Inherited Gift

Dr. Joseph Fagin was the favorite gynecologist of the hospital's staff. He was also unquestionably brilliant. When he had finished his residency, he had applied for work with Saba Pharmaceuticals. The day he applied, there were eleven others applying who shared his nearly perfect credentials. The woman who interviewed him for Saba was extremely impressed with Joseph, and a year later, she married him. When he decided to leave Saba, Joseph looked for a hospital position. He became part of the new Seaside hospital's staff at the very beginning.

Dr. Fagin smiled as he looked up from Abby's chart and at his patient. "It's just as we both thought, Abby. You have been experiencing Braxton Hicks contractions — false labor — off and on throughout this second pregnancy of yours. This time they were stronger, but a false alarm nonetheless." He turned to Andy. "Don't worry. Other than needing to get a little more rest, she's doing fine. It should be a few more weeks."

Andy nodded. "Good. We agreed yesterday that I will take over shopping duties, and I'll be cooking more of our meals. I need the practice." He grinned.

Abby laughed. "At least Trina taught you how to boil water without burning it."

"Trina?" Joe looked at her.

She continued to smile. "My mother-in-law - she's the best one I could have ever hoped for."

"Oh, okay, be sure to call me if you have any

concerns at any time. Meanwhile, I have three patients upstairs that I need to check on. I'll see you." The gynecologist went out.

Andy bent down and kissed Abby. "Do you need me to drive you home?"

"No, Debbie followed me down. She's in the cafeteria getting coffee. She should be back any minute."

Andy nodded. "Okay, I'll see you this evening. I'm going to stop and get groceries on the way home. I'm fixing lime and paprika game hens with rice, unless you insist on starting them before I get home."

"Cornish hens are easy to fix, and Toby will be hungry when you get home, so I'll get things started. I'll see you later."

"Right." He winked. "See you later, sexy!" He walked out. As he walked away, he saw John Cochran standing at the nurses' station. "Hey, John, how's it going?"

The surgeon smiled. "Fine, so far, Andy. I've witnessed a miracle that you'll appreciate."

"Really? What's that?"

"Not what, but who, Andy, and it is someone you know. Do you remember calling on your friend from junior high days last week?"

"Sure! I hadn't seen Rita for thirty years. I did not get a chance to get back to her before her surgery."

"Right, and I told you that she wanted tests repeated before I did her surgery. Well, when I re-did the tests her cancer had totally disappeared. She went home without having surgery. I spent a half hour talking with her insurance agent this morning, explaining what happened."

Andy stood there, stunned. "Wow. Praise God!"

"Amen." He paused. "In recent years, my wife,

Andrea, and I had not been going to church much. Because of that miracle, this last Sunday we worshiped together, and we plan to get back into nurturing our faith in God with each other."

"Fantastic! That's great news too!" He paused. "I've got to get back to the office, John, but did you hear that we have a site for a parking lot now?"

"Really? Where?"

"Do you remember the house on Elm Street that kids like to say is haunted?"

"Sure, but a single lot would not be big enough for the hospital's needs."

"True, but the late Dandy Cooper also owned the lots on either side that he never put houses on. The three large lots, plus an alley easement behind them will give us enough room, if we can work out the legalities and financing. I have both a realtor and an architect working on the project. Anyway, I'd better get going."

"It sounds terrific. I'll see you later."

Andy walked rapidly back to his office, his mind filled with hundreds of fleeting images from the past. Going in, he spoke with his secretary, who glanced at him with a quizzical look. "Janet, Abby's fine, it was just some early contractions. See if you can get Pastor Paul McMasters on the phone, will you?"

"Sure." She reached for her revolving directory.

Andy walked into his office, closed the door, and hung up his coat. As he sat down, his phone rang. "Yes?"

"Paul McMasters is on line 1."

"Thank you, Janet." He paused. "Hi, Pastor Paul. By any chance are you going to be in your office at around 4:30 this afternoon?"

There was a pause. "Sure, Andy, what's going on?"

"Well, with my Dad gone, I need to talk to you about what Mom refers to as his special gift."

"Okay. I'll see you later."

"Yeah, see you later." He hung up.

The rest of the afternoon went by in a blur. Even when he gazed out his office window and saw people walking toward the beach, his thoughts were a jumble of his Dad, his Mom, and hundreds of incidents during his lifetime. As he drove, he remembered when John Beek was struck by lightning in the church parking lot, and Huck put his hand on John's burned face and prayed. A moment later, the two of them stood up, and John was just a little dazed. Andy smiled with the memory.

It was a short drive from the hospital to Andy and Abby's church. It was an imposing building that faced east on Ximeno Street, styled after a cathedral in Mexico, but smaller. The pastor's office was on the south side, near the parking lot. On the north side was a day-care center.

He parked near the pastor's office door and went in. "Hi, Pastor Paul, thanks for seeing me on short notice." He sat down, and so did the pastor.

Pastor Paul was too short for his weight because he enjoyed more food than necessary. His gray hair was thinning, but his quick brown eyes reflected his intelligence even while his voice had a ring of compassion. He smiled.

Andy made himself comfortable. "This morning, one of the surgeons at the hospital told me of a miraculous healing of an old friend of mine, who suddenly had all of her cancer disappear."

The pastor nodded. "After I did your Dad's memorial service a few weeks ago, I wondered when I would be having a conversation with you about this kind of thing."

"Yeah, Mom and Dad talked a lot about prayer while we were eating when I was growing up. Dad gave me lessons on being a prayer warrior. Do you remember how Dad used to pray?"

"Of course, I do. Whenever I saw on the schedule that Huck was going to pray during a worship service, I was careful to make my sermon just a bit shorter. His prayers were often long, but no one ever complained about it, and most looked forward to his prayers."

Andy nodded. That's true. As I recently told friends, Dad was almost casual when he was praying, but it was also intimate, reverential, and humble. He considered Jesus his best friend and constant companion - not merely his Savior." As the pastor nodded, Andy went on. "He could definitely pray long prayers that didn't seem long."

Pastor Paul smiled. "You may remember David Cole, the elder that went home to heaven last year. He used to say that when your Dad prayed, it was as though he had his head resting on Christ's shoulder, and he was running his fingers through the Lord's hair."

Andy nodded. "Whenever people asked Huck to pray for them, he often asked permission and then put his hand on their shoulder or on top of their head as he prayed. Many people said that they felt warm while he was praying for them, and a few said that the warmth flowed from his hand. Mom says that warmth brought healing. Now, I'm wondering if somehow I've inherited that touch - or something. If I have, it seems like an unusual gift."

The pastor was thoughtful. "To refer to this phenomenon in terms of a touch makes it sound like magic rather than something from God. Many schools of so-called energy healing exist, using many names, including spiritual healing, therapeutic touch, and other names. Alleged transcendent healing occurs non-denominationally and ecumenically. People associated with it do not see traditional religion as a prerequisite for effecting cures. Faith's healing usually happens in a religious setting, but that's not the case with you and your Dad."

"It's not?"

"No, in this case, we're talking about the results of prayer. The effectiveness of prayer has been studied world-wide, beginning in the late nineteenth century. It is the most common supplement to mainstream medicine. Double-blind scientific studies have been conducted on several occasions, but the results have been inconclusive. Personally, I think that since God is spirit, not matter and energy, there can never be a conclusive scientific study on the subject. Science does not have the tools to study anything not associated with matter, energy, space, and time. After all, the results of effective prayer are the work of the Holy Spirit."

Andy spoke quietly. "Dad once told me that all any of us can do is serve God with prayer and leave the rest to divine control."

Pastor Paul nodded. "There have been very few carefully monitored studies of prayer. I've read the results of a couple of them. I've been encouraged, but I believe in the power of prayer anyway. Like I said before, I don't think we'll ever get repeatable and conclusive results."

Andy stood up. "This has been helpful. You've given me a lot to think about. Thanks for your time, Pastor Paul." He extended his hand.

They shook hands. "You're welcome. I probably

don't need to say this, but no one expects you to be like Huck. I, for one, simply expect you to be yourself."

Andy smiled. "Thanks. I'll see you Sunday." He turned and walked out. After getting into his car, Andy closed his eyes. "Thank you Lord. I'll say more thanks later when I'm praying with Abby. I don't know what the future holds, but I trust you."

+ + +

Friday evening, Abby and Andy arranged for a babysitter and went to Debbie and Mike's home for dinner. After supper, they sat down with their coffee and tea to talk. Mike asked about the future parking lot. "Where's the property for the parking lot you've talked about?"

Andy smiled. "It is a different piece of property than the one I told you about when we talked a couple of weeks ago. That fell through. This is the Dandy Cooper place on Elm Street, the one we kids used to think was haunted. Mr. Cooper lived there all of his life, and he owned both the house and the lots either side of it. It's less than a block from the hospital."

Abby nodded. "There's an old flood control conduit underground that connects the two properties too."

Debbie smiled. "That sounds terrific. Mike and I will probably be spending some time at the hospital soon. Mike's been told that he may have prostate cancer."

Abby took a positive attitude. "A lot has changed since my own Dad had prostate cancer. You'll know more after your tests."

Debbie nodded. "Just keep us in your prayers, won't you?"

"Of course, course we will." Abby nodded also.

Andy was quiet. "We'll do that, but why not start now?" He took Abby's hand, and he reached out to take

31

Mike's hand. Mike and Debbie made the circle complete. "I'll pray silently for a minute or so, and Abby, you close when you think it's time."

"Okay." The silence lasted several minutes. Abby's prayer was barely above a whisper. "Father, thank you for moving among us, and thank you for letting us feel your spirit moving over and through us. Thank you, Jesus, for forgiving us and redeeming us. In the power of your name, we pray. Amen."

They all sat back in their seats. Debbie asked, "This may sound strange, but what just happened? Was the warmth I felt the Holy Spirit? Did you feel it, Mike?"

Mike nodded. "I felt warm all over, and there was an intense and fiery heat down low in my body. It didn't hurt, but it was intense."

Andy looked directly at his friend. "If it was the presence and power of the Holy Spirit you felt, then you are experiencing its healing. If you are healed, and you feel the need to talk about it with others, please do not connect Abby and I to your healing. Please just say that you got together with some friends for prayer. You can talk about what happened tonight without naming who was here. Can you do that, please?" They both nodded.

Abby smiled. "Thanks. When you hear of someone wanting prayer, feel free to invite us to whatever gathering for prayer may be appropriate, but it would be better if others were there as well."

Andy nodded. "I'm not my Dad. I am my own person. Dad did public prayers which were memorable and helped many people. I do not have Dad's eloquence with public prayer."

Mike nodded. "Debbie and I will respect your privacy, won't we Debbie?"

"Absolutely!"

"If God has cured me, we won't hide it, but we can talk about prayer without naming names."

"Good." Abby scowled. "My little man inside of me just kicked!"

Andy smiled. "Our time grows closer. Abby, I don't think I told you, but I had a phone call today from a woman named Bobbi Zealand."

"Who is she?"

"She's the manager for Richard and Char Donovan."

Mike sat up straighter. "Aren't they the keyboard artists who live up on Signal Hill? Didn't they predict the eruption of the Yellowstone caldera into a volcano — and the nuclear winter that followed?" [For that story, read *Casting Lots*, ©2015]

Andy nodded. "That's correct. Before the cold and dark years began, they predicted both the eruption and the winter because they practice casting lots to determine God's will. They became known as prophets, and they helped our government deal with that seven-year winter."

Debbie grinned. "Mike and I met them! They did an Easter worship service at Staples Center a few years ago, and we chatted very briefly afterward with them. They are nice people, about our age. He does solo concerts of classical piano works, but when they perform together, they do just about every kind of music. She's incredible on an electronic keyboard."

Andy nodded. "Have you heard of the *Magnificent Seven* music group? Abby and I have several of their CD's"

Mike nodded. "Debbie and I haven't heard them in person, but we've seen some of their music videos. Why? How are they connected with the Donovans?"

Andy smiled. "Bobbi Zealand had to explain that to

33

me. About two years after the Yellowstone eruption, the Donovans performed in Memphis. During the intermission, they told the audience how they had cast lots to determine God's will, and that they were going to do something very risky. They were going to Anchorage."

Abby smiled. "We have an amazing CD of that concert."

Andy held up a hand. "You're getting ahead of me, Abby. After they made that announcement, when they reached their next stop, they had telegrams from eight musicians who had been in Memphis that wanted to join them in Anchorage. One of the eight had to drop out due to a family situation, so the Donovans plus the remaining seven went to Anchorage."

Debbie smiled. "So what happened?"

"Evidently, because all of them are such pros, they talked about touring the whole country together. When the Donovans declined because of other engagements, the result was the music group known as *The Magnificent Seven*. That happened just over ten years ago. They have decided to re-unite with the Donovans for a benefit concert at our Long Beach Convention Center. The proceeds will help pay for the hospital's new parking lot. As Richard Donovan likes to say, 'All that God does, God does well.' Now, I'm hoping we can get the Dandy Cooper property at a good price, and that the city will approve the project there,"

+ + +

On Monday morning, Andy had no sooner sat down at his desk, then his phone rang, and he picked up the receiver. "Yes?"

"Greg Hosmar is on line one."

"Thanks." He pushed a button. "Good morning, Greg, how was your weekend?"

"It was busy, as usual, Andy. I'm taking today and tomorrow off. I'm calling to let you know that the city acquired the Cooper property late on Friday for the hospital's parking garage, after the council dealt with some red tape."

"That's great! Have you told Tom Elliott?"

"The council saw some preliminary drawings he had given them, so that's why things are moving so fast. Tom is starting on the blueprints this week."

"Fantastic! This is great news. Are you and your wife going to take off for a few days?"

"Yeah, I think we'll head north, up to see friends in Carpentaria. Their house is only about a hundred miles north of here, right on the coast."

"Good! Enjoy yourselves. I'll see ya when you get back!"

"Yeah. Bye."

Andy punched his mother's number on the phone. "Good morning, Mom."

"Good morning, Andy, what's up?"

"Do you remember that old mansion on Elm Street that we kids used to set up as a haunted house every Halloween?"

"Sure! Did you know Huck and I helped get that tradition started?"

"No! Really?"

"Yes! Huck knew Dandy for a long time. Right after you were born, Dandy and Huck were having lunch together, and somehow they came up with the idea of decorating Dandy's house to look like it was haunted. That first year, both your Dad and I were really impressed with how the house looked. I told Dandy, – as a joke, mind you – that if it looked that way all year, we could make it look even scarier the next Halloween. We laughed about it, but the idea appealed to Dandy for some reason."

Andy laughed. "Wow, Mom, I'm surprised. I've never heard that story before."

His mother laughed too. "You've not once heard it because your Dad and I never brought it up again. It was sort of an inside joke until now. Why are you asking about it?"

"You know that Dandy Cooper died not long ago, don't you?"

"Yes, I saw it in the paper. Why?"

"If legalities can be worked out, it looks like that property, along with the lots north and south of it, which Mr. Cooper also owned, will become the site of the new multilevel parking lot for the hospital."

"That's terrific, son. I'll add this to my prayer list."

"Good. I just thought you would like to know. I'll see you Sunday! I love you!"

"I love you, too, Andy." The connection ended.

4.
Good News Friends

Sitting in Dr. Yoshpe's office, Mike and Debby talked quietly until the doctor walked in. "I have good news for you - almost unbelievable news. Mike, your PSA test is back to normal. It has gone from a score of 26 down to 3. That is miraculous, though the PSA is not notably reliable. Your digital rectal exam a few minutes ago, as I told you, felt normal. Your biopsy indicates no evidence of cancer in your prostate. I recommend that we do a prostate MRI in a year, okay?"

Both Mike and Debbie were smiling. Mike nodded. "I like the idea of the MRI rather than another biopsy. All of this is an answer to prayer, isn't it, Debbie?"

She nodded. "Dr. Yoshpe, we prayed about this with friends last week, and, frankly, I'm not surprised that Mike's tests are negative. Mike and I are people of faith."

The doctor nodded and pushed his glasses further up on his nose. "I remember you telling me that you're active in a church. I am a Christian, but I do not go to church as often as I should. My wife goes and takes our children, though." He paused. "I'll have Julie schedule that MRI for you." He stood up. "I'm glad this turned out so well. Any time you have a concern, feel free to call."

"Thank you, Dr. Yoshpe." Mike extended his hand. "Thank you very much. God bless you."

"Thank you." He showed them the door.

+ + +

Later that week, Andy was leaning back in his office chair while talking on the phone with Char Donovan. "When you and Richard first got on the nightly news because of your prophecy concerning the volcano in Yellowstone, I also wondered about having someone in our family history named Donovan. I asked my Dad about it. He wondered if one of Richard's great-great-grandparents was Walter Franklyn Hickman. If so, he was my granduncle on my mother's side. I was born when my Dad was seventy-one."

Char Donovan was startled. "Yikes! Really?"

Andy smiled. "It's absolutely true, Char. When my Mom asked my Dad to marry her, she was twenty-two and Dad was seventy."

"Wow! That is amazing. To answer your earlier question, at the moment Richard is downstairs practicing for performances next week in Los Angeles. We want you and your wife to come over some evening for dinner so that we can get better acquainted. Would this coming Sunday evening be a good time?"

"Let me look at my calendar. I'll put you on hold just briefly." He pressed hold and then the intercom button. "Janet, do Abby and I have anything on our calendar for Sunday evening?"

"No, you're both free for the day."

"Put us down for dinner with Char and Richard Donovan."

"Okay."

He pushed the line one button. "I checked with my secretary, and it's all clear. I will tell Abby when I see her this evening. She's eight months along with our second child. What time will you expect us?"

"Make it six. How old is your first child?"

"Toby is a toddler, almost two."

"Terrific! Bring him along. Our two kids will love to play with him. In addition, if you and Abby would enjoy our indoor hot tub and pool, you're welcome to use it. We'll eat at about seven, okay?"

"This sounds terrific! We will look forward to it. See you then."

"Until then." He and Char disconnected.

He pushed the intercom button. "Janet, get Abby on the phone for me, please."

Andy hung up and leaned back in his chair.

"Abby is on line one, Andy," Janet called out.

"Thanks." He picked up the phone. "Hey, beautiful, how are you doing this afternoon?"

"Things have been pretty quiet. I'm getting sick of watching so much television and videos, but I want to go to a full term."

"I do too, dear. Listen, you and I have been invited to dinner with Char and Richard Donovan, who live up on Signal Hill."

"Are you talking about the musicians?"

"It's the same couple. He is performing with the Los Angeles Philharmonic this coming week, and Char Donovan has asked us to join them for dinner on Sunday evening. They are going to be doing a benefit concert for the hospital along with the group called 'The Magnificent Seven.' For Sunday evening, she says her kids will love playing with Toby, and if we want to bring our swim suits, they have an indoor pool and hot tub."

"Oooh. I would love to walk around in a pool. With buoyancy, I won't be carrying this weight around while I'm in the pool."

Andy chuckled. "I'm sure you'll enjoy that! We're to be there at six, and we'll eat at seven."

"I'm putting it on our kitchen calendar. I assume

that Janet has your hospital calendar clear."

"Exactly, I love you, Abby. I'll see you later."

"I love you too. Bye."

+ + +

Saturday evening, Richard Donovan pulled their SUV into their driveway, and as Char got out on the other side, Richard closed his door and looked up at the sky. As she closed her door and pushed the button to lock the doors, she glanced over at Richard. "It's late. The kids are probably asleep." She went around the car, joined her husband, and put her arm around him. "The concerts went well this weekend, and it's a nice night. Shall we grab a couple of chairs and do some stargazing?"

Richard shook his head as he put his arm around her. "We could, but I have a need to go to my knees right now. Let's go get the kids from Rita, get them tucked in here at home, and then go and kneel on our *prie-dieu* upstairs, okay?"

"Okay." Holding hands, they walked across the street to Jim and Rita's house and rang the bell.

The door opened, and Rita spoke quietly. "Hi! How did the concert go?"

Char smiled at her friend. "Richard's performance was fine, and the orchestra was really polished."

Richard nodded. "Afterward, we got to chat with the governor for about five minutes. I don't think I'm prejudiced when I say that it seems like Republicans have a finer appreciation for Beethoven and Chopin than Democrats do."

Rita laughed. "Richard, that somehow doesn't surprise me." She paused. "The kids have all been asleep for a couple of hours now. Why don't you let them stay here tonight? Jim and I can bring them over first thing in the morning, in time to go to church."

Jim came around the corner from the dining room. "Hey, you two! Yeah! We'll fix breakfast for them and bring them over around eight, okay?"

Char smiled. "That will be great! Richard and I can use some alone time." She glanced up at Richard.

"Yeah, this will work out great! Tomorrow after lunch, Char and I can treat you and your kids to a movie with us, okay?" Richard shook Jim's hand, and he nodded.

Rita gave Char a hug. "See you tomorrow morning, you two!"

Almost together, Char and Richard said, "Good night!" They turned and left.

As they crossed the street, Richard looked down at Char. "This works out great."

"Right. We have to be careful, though, with our time in the theater. We're having Andy and Abby Hickman over for dinner tomorrow, remember?" Richard nodded as he unlocked the front door and went in. As he moved toward the stairs, Char let go of his hand. "I'm going to take some ribs out of the freezer for tomorrow. You go ahead. I'll be right up."

Richard climbed the stairs and went to their master bedroom in the front of the house. They had their *prie-dieu* several feet from the front window so that when they knelt there they could look out over the city without the neighbors seeing them from below.

He stood there, looking out, until Char quietly came in and stood beside him. She looked at him. "It seems like you've been emotionally in your man-cave ever since you took your bows at the end of the concert this evening. Even when we were talking with the governor, it seemed like you were somewhere else."

He nodded. "Do you remember that first time we were in Tokyo, and what I told you about my encore?"

Char closed her eyes. "I think you said, ' I suddenly felt a fire inside of me, and hardly without thinking about it, I plunged into that Bach-Busoni.' Tonight you surprised me by playing Debussy's *L'Isle Joyeuse.* I don't think you've done that since our tour stop in Omaha during that long winter."

He nodded. "I felt that fire again tonight. Maybe God is trying to get our attention. Let's pray about it, and if we need to, we can cast lots tonight before we go to bed."

They knelt on the kneeler, and time passed quickly. It was shortly before 2:00 AM when they finished praying and casting lots, and they turned off the light.

+ + +

Sunday night, Andy parked their SUV at the top of Signal Hill in front of Richard and Char's house. As a very pregnant Abby began to maneuver herself out, Andy went around and got Toby out of his child's seat. They started up the sidewalk.

Now in their thirties, Richard and Char Donovan were often in the public's eye. Just after they got married, they prophesied without error that the Yellowstone Caldera would erupt and become a volcano. Just as accurately, they predicted that there would be a worldwide winter that would last nearly seven years. Shortly after returning from their honeymoon, they had purchased this house.

The front door opened, and Char Donovan greeted them with a smile. "Good evening and welcome! I'm Char Donovan."

The pianist appeared next to her, just as Andy, Abby, and Toby arrived at the door. "Hi! I'm Richard

42

Donovan - come on in."

As they came in, all three of the Hickmans took in the massive entry area, the spiral staircase, and the great room. Abby smiled, looking down at their son holding her hand. "This is Toby." She paused, looking around. "Your house is so beautiful - you have quite a home here!"

Char nodded. "Thank you. Richard and I have no doubt that God led us to this place. We can tell you that story another time." She turned to look up the stairway and called out. "Richie! Meghan! Come down! The Hickmans are here!"

They could hear the kids thudding along the upstairs hallway and down the stairs. Richard looked up. "Slow down, kids, you know better!"

As Toby looked up the stairs, he grinned. "Hi! I'm Toby!"

"I'm Meghan!"

"I'm Richie."

As they all moved towards the great room, Richie and Meghan took Toby towards the home theater. Delicious aromas were coming from the kitchen as the adults sat down. Andy pointed towards the pianos. "It didn't occur to me that you would have two pianos, but I guess if you're going to rehearse together its necessary."

Richard nodded. "The larger one was given to me as a bonus to our fee when we played in Japan the first time. Just after the Yellowstone eruption, Sony sponsored two concerts. That piano was the one supplied for playing with a symphony orchestra, and afterward they shipped it home with us. When the movers arrived with it, we moved over the Yamaha digital keyboard that is now next to it."

Char nodded. "When we do the benefit concert for

your hospital, Richard will play an acoustic piano, and I'll be on a digital keyboard. The Magnificent Seven' will be on either side of us. We'll be set up the same way as we did our previous concert in Anchorage just after Yellowstone's caldera erupted."

Abby's eyes got big. "Andy and I discussed that earlier."

Char nodded. "When our piston-prop plane landed it was about 50 below zero. Elmendorf–Richardson in Anchorage is an amalgamation of Elmendorf Air Force Base and the Army's Fort Richardson. It was our one and only performance with the seven musicians who had seen our performance in Nashville. Richard and I performed with Tom Dobbins, Lou Mendez, Lori Simpson, Angel Madison, Bob Presley, Bill Jones, and Rick Stevens in a large hanger. We've still got a Blu-ray concert disk of that concert in circulation."

Richard nodded. "It was a lot of fun. Afterward, the others suggested that the nine of us do a train tour, but we had to decline. Since then, they have been performing as the 'Magnificent Seven" periodically along with their individual performances. This benefit concert gives the nine of us a chance to play together again for the first time since Anchorage." He paused. "Tell us about this parking garage project."

He was thoughtful. "It's been an ongoing struggle since the hospital opened, and a perpetual source of complaining from staff and patients alike. I constantly have to explain to people that we are working on the problem. Up until now, we have operated shuttles from other lots in the downtown area. Recently, a former patient indirectly provided three large lots. It is just a block over from the hospital, and there is an old underground flood control viaduct that connects the

44

new property to the hospital. Blueprints for a multilevel parking garage were approved this week, and construction will begin soon. We hope. Now it is a matter of raising the money. Your benefit concert will help with that. Abby and I were talking today about how the nine of you first got together for that concert in Anchorage. It would seem that this will be a reunion."

Char nodded. "That's right. We'll do some of the music that we did in Anchorage of course, but performing as the "Magnificent Seven," they have been doing their own versions of music that Richard and I have done in Tokyo, Los Angeles, and San Diego. We have cleared our schedules so that we have three days to work out the kinks and rehearse some stuff that will be totally new. This benefit will be recorded for audio CD's, Blu-ray disks, and DVDs, and the profits will later go to the hospital. The Seven insisted on that, and we agreed."

Andy grinned. "That will be great!"

Richard became serious. "In our evening prayers last evening, we felt the need to cast lots for both the benefit concert and the two of you."

Abby was stunned. "For us?"

"Yes." Char nodded.

"We know that God holds the future, of course," Richard continued, "but we have come to the conclusion that the two of you are going to become part of something much larger than the hospital."

Now Andy was stunned. "How?"

"We don't know, but we are certain of it," said Char. "Andy, do you have what some call a spiritual gift?"

He was silent and thoughtful. Abby looked at her husband. "Go ahead, Andy, I think you should tell them about it. Tell them about Huck too."

Andy smiled. "I can always talk about Dad."

Richard smiled. "Your Dad's name was Huck?"

Andy nodded. "Yeah, he and I had the same name, but that was his nickname. Our son playing with your kids is the ninth Andrew Tobias Hickman, but we're calling him Toby. Huck was the seventh, but few people knew him by his full legal name. Anyway, Huck was seventy and my Mom was twenty-two when they met and got married."

Char's eyes were wide. "You mentioned that the other day!"

"Yeah, and as to how God set them up, I can tell you about it some other time. Dad was a pastor before he retired just before he met Mom. Many people talked about Dad's prayers in church. As a prayer warrior, he prayed with a sense of respectful but personal intimacy that everyone loved. A few people talked about something else, though." He paused, and Abby nodded. "When Mom and Dad prayed for people, something seemed to happen. Even Mom says that she could feel warmth flowing over her and through her, and some of those they prayed with said they experienced the same thing. When Dad prayed for someone, he usually asked permission to put his hand on their shoulder or on their head while he prayed."

"So he had a healing touch?"

Andy shook his head. "I don't want to put a label on it. I had a talk with my pastor about Dad recently. He said that to speak about the phenomenon in terms of touch could make it sound like magic to some people. He talked about the terms 'spiritual healing' and 'faith healing,' but he said that the terms did not seem to apply to my Dad."

Char nodded. "Go on."

46

"Recently, there have been a few instances where this phenomenon occurred with me. It seems as though God is using me in a special way, but I am uncomfortable putting a label on it. The two of you are only the second couple we've told about it. We don't want in any way to advertise the phenomena, and Abby and I don't even invite discussion, because we don't pretend to know what God is doing."

Richard smiled. "When I was in the ninth grade, I started casting lots but did not tell anyone about it. When Char and I got married, I did not want to keep it a secret, and I told her about it on our honeymoon. It quickly became something we did several times a week and still do. I don't think we would have told very many others about what we were doing if it weren't for an email we sent to warn our friends about the coming eruption at Yellowstone."

Char laughed. "We were in an airport, and we forgot to use 'blind carbon copy' and used just 'carbon copy' instead."

Andy smiled. "Recently, I talked to my pastor about my Dad and about how God seems to be starting to use me. I cannot think of this as a special touch, except in terms of God's choosing to touch me and use me. I also don't want to think of what is happening in terms of spiritual healing or faith healing. All of it just seems different to me."

Char smiled. "I think I understand what you're saying, Andy. ... Abby, have you decided on a name for your latest child?"

Abby nodded. "Andy and I have had quite a few discussions, and we've decided upon naming him Joseph Andrew Hickman, and we'll call him Joey."

"So you know it's going to be a boy?" asked

Richard.

Abby nodded. "Yes."

+ + +

Down the hill in Long Beach, Andy's Mom had just finished some ice cream drenched in dark chocolate after her dinner. After putting her dishes in the dishwasher, she went to the living room and sat down in the overstuffed rocking chair that Huck used to enjoy. Staring at an out-of-focus spot on the front door, she spoke softly. "Father, I'm so grateful that I can sense your presence whenever I seek you. Huck taught me so very much about good effective prayer. Since Andy and Abby are meeting with the Donovans this evening, I lift them up to you in prayer, that your will be done both in their lives and with the parking garage project."

Trina paused, closed her eyes, and then she opened them again. "As you know, Lord, this afternoon I was looking for something in Huck's desk, and I came across his intercessory prayer list. He used to revise it and print out a new version between Christmas and New Year's every year, but you know that. Anyway, I forgot how big the list is, Lord! There are hundreds – maybe thousands – of names, Lord! When we scattered Huck's ashes, we talked so much about his prayers. I did not mention the list to Mike and Debbie, and I wonder why. I think I want to do what Huck did. Each morning he would pray on behalf of several dozens of the people on his list. I want to continue that. Tomorrow, Lord, please help me clean the list up, taking out the names of people who died last year, and please help me think of those who should be added to the list. In Jesus' name I ask, Amen."

She got up from the rocker, went to the front door, opened it, and stood there, looking out through the

48

screen door. "I hope I'm not biting off more than I can chew," she murmured.

+ + +

Across town in Recreation Park, Rita McLaughlin was jogging. Her breast caner diagnosis and miracle healing were now but a memory. Up ahead, sitting on a bench, was a man who looked vaguely familiar. She stopped. "Danny? Danny Webster?"

He looked up, puzzled, and then began to smile. "Rita? Rita McLaughlin? I've not seen you since the ninth grade at Bancroft!"

"Right!" She sat down on the bench beside him. "It's good to see you! What have you been doing?"

"I'm a Navy Seal. I'm on call 24-7, but I just got back from a mission, so I probably won't get called for at least a week or two. What are you doing?"

"I'm teaching chemistry at Wilson High School. I had a cancer scare last month, but an old friend of ours prayed for me in the hospital, and the cancer disappeared."

"What old friend?"

"Andy Hickman."

"I haven't heard his name since my days at Long Beach City College. He and I were chemistry lab partners a couple of times. He's the administrator at Seaside Hospital now, isn't he?"

Rita nodded. "He told me that when we were at Bancroft, he had a crush on me, but when he asked me out in the ninth grade, I was already going out with Paul Barger."

Danny nodded. "I remember Paul."

She smiled. "Andy married Abby Smith, and they have a boy and another on the way." She paused. "These last few days, I've been wondering what would

49

have happened if I had started dating Andy instead of Paul."

"Did anything develop between you and Paul?"

"No. I've never done well in the romance department. I was engaged to Sid Underwood, but just before we were to be married, he told me that he had asked someone else to marry him, and they had already eloped the previous weekend."

"Ouch! That must have been painful."

Rita nodded. "Yes, but that was nine years ago, and they live in Australia now. I don't miss him a bit!"

Danny looked at his watch. "It's past noon. Would you like to have lunch?"

Rita cocked her head, and then she smiled. "Sure!"

5.
Concert and Zoo

A little over two months later, the Long Beach Arena was packed with more than 13,000 people. While Andy had a seat reserved close to the stage, Abby was in a large nearby room with a huge 4K video display and surround sound. While Abby watched, the baby, Joey, was asleep. He was born three weeks earlier. Toby was playing with some toys in a corner. Abby had previously decided to isolate herself with the baby and Toby, not to disturb others at the concert.

Because of this, Andy had told the Arena staff that other mothers with young children were welcome to enjoy the concert in the "cry room" with his wife. Their friends, Mike and Debby, were with Abby because the Arena had sold out so quickly that they had been unable to get seats.

On the Arena floor, the curtain was down, and Andy's phone vibrated. He looked at the expected message, and he took a deep breath and let it out. Then he stood up, walked up a short stair onto the stage, and faced the audience. His wireless mike had been previously tested and adjusted. "Good evening, everyone." The arena became much quieter. "My name is Andy Hickman, and I'm the Administrator for Seaside Hospital here in Long Beach. As most of you know, tonight's reunion concert is a benefit for the new much-needed multilevel parking garage that is being built near the hospital. The City of Long Beach is providing the Arena and paying the arena staff. The musicians are all donating their fees. Every penny of every ticket is helping pay for the parking garage."

Applause began, and soon the entire audience was on its feet with applause and whistles. After about thirty seconds, he held up his hand for quiet. "It is now my privilege and honor to introduce Char and Richard Donovan with 'The Magnificent Seven!'"

As Andy made his way back to his seat, the curtain went up, the lights came up, and the concert began. As Andy went down the stairs, he turned and paused next to the edge of the stage. No one seemed to notice as Andy put his hand on the edge of the stage and tilted his head back with his eyes closed. On stage, Char began to grin, and her husband glanced up to see his wife smiling. She tipped her head towards Andy. Richard looked over at the administrator, and began to smile with his wife. When Andy opened his eyes and began to clap with the rhythm of the music, the two keyboard artists turned all of their attention back to their performances with the others. The audience remained on its feet throughout the first set.

After nearly an hour, Richard announced, "There will now be a fourteen-and-a-half-minute intermission." There was scattered laughter. While the Donovans and The Magnificent Seven left the stage to take their break, nearly two hundred teenagers gathered on risers on the stage area behind the instrumentalists. The second set began with a series of five Christian praise music songs, with the teens singing their hearts out. With the lyrics displayed on the large 4K video screen above the stage, the audience sang along. When that set was over, most of the teens sat down where they had been standing. The rest sat on chairs at the sides of the stage.

The total performance was just over 150 minutes. After two encores, they called it a night.

Andy went up the stairs to thank Richard, Char, and the others personally. As he approached, Richard grinned at him. "Andy, we did our thing, but you evidently did your thing as well."

"Meaning?"

"My beloved Char saw you as we began playing, and she began to smile. I looked to see where she was looking."

Char walked up and put her arm through Richard's. "Yes! I knew what you were doing because I first saw Richard do that in Tokyo more than ten years ago. He unexpectedly paused to pray just before doing an encore."

Andy was perplexed. "Really? I did not plan to pray at the bottom of the stairs, but it just seemed to happen. I hope it wasn't distracting."

Richard laughed. "Distracting? I wouldn't describe it that way. I think God was using you. Holy power seemed to flow through all of us on stage. Two of the others mentioned it. This was truly a special night, and we're all glad we were here."

Andy nodded. "I think at least 13,000 others were blessed tonight, whether they know it or not. Thanks again to all of you," Andy's eyes swept all the musicians, "for donating your time and money to this."

A tall, portly man walked up. "Hi, my name is Tom Dobbins. I guess you're Andy Hickman."

Andy nodded. "I am. It's good to meet you."

"It's a privilege for me to meet you, sir. After talking with Richard during the intermission, I gather that you're the one responsible for something that happened to me tonight."

Andy was stunned. "What's that?"

Tom spoke quietly. "When we agreed to do this concert, I thought it might be my last. For the last year, I've been dealing with severe osteoarthritis in my hands. I thought I was going to have to retire early. As we began the first song, I was struggling to maintain good technique on my twelve-string and suddenly I felt warmth flowing through me. Then all of my symptoms disappeared, and they have not come back."

Andy's eyes were big. "Praise God! I hope you'll tell your story to anyone who will listen, but please don't connect me with what happened. I don't want the notoriety, okay?"

Tom nodded. "You've got it. I'll honor that, of course." He turned to some gathering people to sign autographs.

Char touched Andy's arm. "I think God's spirit touched the teenagers as well, Andy. Never before have I heard kids that age sing that way. It was amazing."

Richard nodded. "I agree. Andy, check your schedule both at the hospital and with Abby. Char and I want you two to join us for Bible study on Monday evening."

Andy nodded. Abby approached as Richard spoke. "Did you say Monday? I know our calendar's clear, so unless there's something on the hospital's calendar, we'll be there."

Char smiled. "Good. Dinner for everyone is always at 6:00, and we start our study at 7:00."

Abby shook her head. "We don't want to impose upon you for dinner again. We want to take the two of you out sometime."

Char nodded. "We'll take a rain check on that. Richard and I have been having dinner and Bible study in our home three nights a week, for our whole Bible study group, when we are not on tour, ever since shortly after we moved here. Please join us. It will not be an imposition."

Andy nodded. "Okay. We'll see you Monday." He and Abby, along with baby Joey, began circulating among the others back stage. It was a long night.

+ + +

Time seemed to pass quickly for the Hickmans and Donovans. Many months passed as Andy and Abby became regular attendees of the Bible studies at the top of Signal Hill, and the children grew rapidly. Andy and Abby created a self-imposed challenge of introducing the Donovans to restaurants that they had never tried. The Bible study group was typically about twenty adults plus all their children. When someone in the study group mentioned a need for healing, they would all hold hands to pray in a circle, and healing would take place. No one questioned it. They simply praised God.

On the Fourth of July, during the summer before four-year-old Joey was to enter kindergarten, the two families decided to go to the Los Angeles Zoo. As they drove north on the freeway, Abby and Andy did not notice the cars that were escorting them at first, but Toby noticed. "Hey, Dad, there are some cars that are always with us, ever since we left Long Beach. What's going on?"

Andy nodded. "Okay. Abby, call Char and see what she says about our apparent escort. This is weird. Now that you mention it, Toby, I do recognize a couple of cars that I saw in Long Beach."

Abby was holding her cell phone to her ear. "Hey, Char. Toby just noticed that we've got some of the same cars around us now that were with us in Long Beach. Have you and Richard noticed?"

Char laughed. "Richard and I are so used to it. We don't often think about it. It's our federal escort, which first started just after our honeymoon. Don't worry about it. They're good people."

"Okay, bye Char." Abby put her phone back in her purse. "It's a federal escort that Richard and Char always have. She says they are so accustomed to it that they don't even think about it much anymore."

"Interesting!" Andy continued to drive silently.

As they pulled into the parking lot, there were oohs and ahhs from the kids in the back seat. Wanting to stay with the Donovans, Andy followed Richard across the parking lot to a drop-off point at the main gate. A man in uniform approached their SUV, and Andy rolled down his window. "Hello, Mr. Hickman, I'm lieutenant Oestricher. I'll take care of your SUV, while you and your family go on in."

Andy nodded. "Thank you." He turned towards the back. "Okay, kids, everybody out. There's parking service for us."

With Richard leading the way, they all approached the main entrance and went in through a VIP gate off to one side. They held their children's hands as they began to tour the zoo. A few people approached Richard or Char for autographs, but the crowds did not bother them.

In the early afternoon, they stopped to have lunch, and the kids ate as though they had not eaten for a week. Andy pointed at the children "With all the pop that the kids are drinking to wash down their lunches, I think we'll probably have to take a restroom break soon."

Abby nodded. "You'd think we never feed them!"

She paused, looking around at the area. "I wonder where the Marines have gone. I don't see them anywhere."

Char nodded. "I love it when they do this. When we are at home on top the hill, Richard and I know that they are somewhere nearby, but we don't see them. They blend into the background."

Richard smiled. "Right, I saw our lieutenant that drove us step into the foliage near the ice cream stand. I can't see him, but I'm certain he's there."

Andy heard Toby sucking air through his straw from the bottom of his drink cup. He looked at the kids. "Has everyone had enough?"

Toby said, "Yeah," and the other kids echoed him.

"Come on, everyone," Andy stood up. "Let's head over to the big cats' area.

As they were crossing a large square, shots rang out. "Hit the deck!" yelled Richard, and everyone but Andy dropped down flat on the ground. Andy knelt. Abby crawled over, knelt beside him, and held his hand. As Andy and Abby touched their foreheads to the pavement, the day suddenly got dark as they heard yelling nearby. There were almost a dozen very loud reports, like canons firing, with flashes of light from several directions.

Suddenly, there was silence. The clouds above them that had been so dark began to break apart. As they lifted their faces, the same lieutenant who had taken care of their car approached Andy and Abby. "We'll take care of cleaning things up here and assisting the police. Where were you going when this happened?"

"We were going to go see the big cats."

"Good. Will you please take your children, along with the Donovan family, and head that way? We need to clear this immediate area of the zoo for a while."

In the distance, they could hear sirens. Andy nodded, and he beaconed to Richard. "Let's go see the big cats." Richard nodded, and the two families started to leave the area.

As they turned a corner, a man in uniform approached them that they had not seen before. He seemed to be of higher rank. "Hello, I'm Captain Jim Sullivan. May I ask you a question, Mr. Hickman?" Andy nodded as the others stopped to listen. "When shots were first fired, everybody laid flat on the ground except you and your wife. The two of you knelt. May I ask why?"

Abby nodded. "We pray about a lot of things, and in a crisis, we're often on our knees."

Andy smiled. "Right. We noticed that, as we were praying things got dark temporarily. There are only a few scattered clouds in the sky now. What happened?"

The captain smiled. "I'm not sure I believe it myself. The shots were from two rival gangs that evidently decided to start a war here at the zoo. Those clouds quickly merged over the zoo, and there were at least a dozen bolts of lighting. There was no rain, let alone thunderstorms, in the weather forecast. Anyway, the lightning bolts struck the shooters, and all of them are dead."

Everyone's eyes grew wide. Andy's mouth dropped open, and then he closed it. "Really? All we did was pray for the safety of those around us. All that God does, God does well."

The captain looked puzzled. "I suppose so. I'm not much of a religious man, but the two of you have given me a lot to think about. Thank you. Enjoy the rest of your zoo visit."

As the captain turned and went, Abby and Andy

looked up and said, "Thanks!" almost simultaneously.

Richard turned to Andy and Abby. "Do you remember what Char and I told you the first time we had dinner together?"

Andy nodded. "You told us that God was going to use us in powerful ways."

Abby nodded. "This is off the wall!"

Joey tugged on Andy's finger. "Dad, can we go see the big cats now?"

Andy nodded. "Sure, son, go take your brother's hand, and the two of you can lead the way - slowly."

As they started down the wide and paved pathway, Char spoke to Abby quietly. "Even though I have confidence in our military escorts, I must admit I was scared spit-less, weren't you?"

Abby was quiet for a moment. "When I first hit the ground I was shaking all over, but then I looked to see where Andy was, and he was about five feet from me, but on his knees. Suddenly, for some reason, I was calm. I crawled over and rose up enough to kneel beside him while I held his hand. His eyes were closed, so I closed mine, and as he leaned forward to become prostrate, I did the same. The darkness surprised me because it was so *incredibly* dark. When the first lightning bolt struck I could feel the heat, but, strangely, I was peaceful."

Char nodded as they continued to walk along. "When Richard and I were on our honeymoon, the first time we cast lots together we were in a chapel in Grand Tetons National Park. I wasn't sure what to expect, but loving Richard, I wanted to join him on his spiritual path. When the two coins Richard used at the time came up either heads-heads or tails-tails every time, I became totally in awe of God. It was a holy kind of fear. As time has passed, and as we have cast lots together repeatedly to determine God's will, well ..." She paused. "I don't think we'll ever take God's will for granted, and we're still in awe of what often happens."

Richard and Andy were walking right behind them. Richard spoke quietly too. "With all of what Char and I have experienced since we got married, I'm right now in awe of what happened less than fifteen minutes ago. I was confident that the soldiers who accompany us could handle everything, but then the sky turned black." They arrived at some benches near the pits where the big cats. "Kids, come and sit here with us!"

Together, they said, "Awww," but they did as they were told.

Andy nodded. "The sky turning black was freaky. When those first shots rang out, and you told everyone to hit the deck, I somehow knew that God was involved. I knelt and surrendered." He paused. "There is something I've been meaning to ask you about."

Richard looked at him. "What's that?"

"Char said something backstage on the night of the hospital benefit concert that got my attention, but I forgot to ask her about it."

Char was sitting on the other side of Richard. "What did I say, Andy?"

"You said that the first time you saw someone close their eyes while looking up was when Richard did it in Tokyo. I gathered that Richard did something then that surprised you."

As Richard chuckled, Char smiled. "You've got that right! Richard and I always plan for encores, but that night Richard surprised me. He unexpectedly played a difficult piece written especially for that piano, and he played it faster and more skillfully than anyone's thought was possible. Richard's done it frequently as an encore ever since."

Just then, a zookeeper approached with a covered cart. Andy stood up. "Joey, hold my hand. Toby, take your mother's hand. Let's watch them feed the cats." They explored the zoo the rest of the day, and when they finally drove home, all the kids were sound asleep.

+ + +

That evening, Mike and Debbie had finished dinner and were watching the evening news. As a commercial concluded, their favorite anchor returned. "Tonight, we've an unusual story to tell from the Los Angeles Zoo and Botanical Gardens. Prudy Garza is there with our story. Prudy?"

"Today, gang warfare broke out here at the Los Angeles Zoo, but it was over just moments after it started. I'm here with Jonathan Chung, chief of security for the zoo. Tell us about what happened, Mr. Chung."

A tall, muscular Asian man explained. "As you said, gang warfare momentarily broke out. Normally, when an emergency happens, we evacuate all the visitors, we shut down the whole zoo, and the police help us deal with whatever problems we face. This time, that was not necessary. There were VIP visitors with us today, and there were several U.S. Marines here as their security detail. When a few shots rang out, someone shouted, 'hit the deck,' and while all the guests in the area either got down or ran away, the Marines took positions to defend the guests. Then the sky got very dark, and there were several bolts of lightning. The gang members who had started the conflict were struck by that lightning, but for some strange reason, no one else was hurt. After some of the Marines saw to it that the area was cleared, we yellow-taped off the area. By the time the police arrived, the rest of the zoo was back to normal operations."

Prudy Garza nodded. "Thank you Mr. Chung." The man walked away, and Ms. Garza gestured to a police officer who appeared to be in her thirties, and in a blue uniform with a cap. "We also have with us Captain Jody Donovan, who was one of the first police officers on the scene. When you arrived, Captain Donovan, what did you see?"

"When I first got here I was approached by Captain Jim Sullivan of the U.S. Marines, and he told me what Mr. Chung just told you. Two marines had helped yellow-tape the area off, and when the crimes investigation unit arrived, they went to work. There were evidently eight young men and three adolescent women killed by the lighting. Six were from one gang and five from another. It will take some time to identify them by anything other than their gang colors because the lightning charred them pretty badly. All of this is doubly strange because there were no storms of any kind in the weather forecast, and there was no rain with the lightning. The thunderheads formed and disbursed rather quickly. Maybe your station's meteorologist can offer some kind of explanation. This is all we know so far."

"Thank you, Captain Donovan. Now, back to the studio."

Mike put the TV on mute. "Andy and Abby were there today. We'll have to call them. Maybe they saw some of this."

Debbie nodded. "Even if they did not hear the shots, we can be sure they heard the thunder. Maybe they saw the lightning too."

+ + +

Captain Jim Sullivan, the Marine in command of the Donovans' security escort at the zoo that day, knocked on Pastor Paul McMasters' door. The door opened, to a smiling, slightly overweight man. "Hello, I'm Jim Sullivan."

"Good afternoon, I'm Pastor Paul McMasters. Come in and make yourself comfortable."

"Thanks!" He sat down.

Pastor Paul sat down and leaned back in his chair. "What can I do for you, Captain Sullivan?"

"First of all, thank you for seeing me this evening. My wife is a Christian and goes to the Baptist church over on Atlantic. I'm not a religious man, but I go to church with my wife from time to time just because she wants me to. This afternoon I had a strange experience. I'm part of a Marine escort watching over Char and Richard Donovan, the musicians. Today, they went with friends and their children to the Los Angeles Zoo. When shots rang out, everyone hit the ground except two people. They knelt in prayer instead. Afterward, I asked them why, and they said that when they're in a crisis, they pray. I've been thinking about their answer ever since. Meanwhile, my team kept our charges away from the media, and zoo officials dealt with those wanting details about the incident. When I got back to the base, I checked the man and woman out, and I learned they go to your church. That's why I'm here."

Pastor Paul sat up straighter in his chair. "They go to this church? Who are they?"

"Andy and Abby Hickman are their names."

Pastor Paul smiled, relaxed, and sat back. "Tell me more about it."

The captain proceeded to tell more of his story. Pastor Paul talked to him about prayer, and he began leading the Captain into a relationship with God through Jesus Christ.

6.
Construction Begins

Six days later, the private dining room at Seaside Hospital was used for a meeting of the hospital's governing board. Andy rapped the gavel, and the meeting came to order. After the board secretary read the minutes from the previous meeting, and the minutes were approved, Andy stood up and passed out a printed progress report for the new parking garage. "As all of you know, the property for the garage was provided by the city, after it was purchased from the estate of the late Dandy Cooper. The closing costs were minimal, as we've previously discussed. Furthermore, as we've earlier discussed, the architectural fee for Tom Elliott was paid for by an anonymous donor." A board member on his right raised her hand. "Yes, Tonia?"

"Do we know who that donor is?"

"'Yes and no' is the necessary answer. When I received the check made out to the hospital, earmarked for the architect's fee, I personally deposited the check into the hospital's account. I had the bank draw a check for the same amount made out to Tom Elliott, and I turned the paperwork over to Wells and Robinson, our accountants. The identity of the donor, per the donor's instructions, is known only by our accountants and me."

"Thank you."

"Since the use of the arena was donated by the city for the benefit concert, and since the musicians are writing off their fees as a business expense, the total receipts from the ticket sales, along with corporate donations, are therefore applied to the anticipated construction costs." There was murmuring. "Yes, the concert is paying for 98.2% of the total cost of the garage."

Several board members nodded their approval. "Fantastic!" said one of them.

"In the box part way down the page, you will see a chart covering our current costs of running the shuttle system to lots up to a mile away. Once the parking garage is finished and in operation, I recommend all but two of the shuttle buses be sold. The income from that, plus the decreased cost of fuel and maintenance for the shuttles, will cover the remaining costs of parking garage construction. After construction is complete, I anticipate that the sales of CD's, DVDs, and Blu-ray disks will cover staffing costs for the garage."

"I move we accept this report and proceed as described," said John Laraway, at the other end of the table.

"I second it," said Tonia.

"Discussion?" Heads were shaking. "All those in favor?"

It was unanimous, and the meeting was adjourned for lunch. As he stood to follow the others to the cafeteria line, Andy looked up and silently said a prayer of thanks. "Friends, I've work to do, so I'll not be joining you for lunch today. Have a great week, everyone!" He waved and went out another door, walking rapidly back to his office.

As he came in, Janet was finishing her lunch. "Everything went as expected, Janet. You'll probably get a copy of the minutes in a couple of days. I've got a project for you. I'll be seeing Richard and Char Donovan tomorrow evening, so I'll thank them again at that time." Janet reached for her notebook and began writing. "Over the next few days, I want to make personal phone calls to everyone in the 'Magnificent Seven.' To save time, call Char Donovan. Tell her you are my secretary, and that you need all those phone numbers. There should not be any problem. You might ask her for the best time to reach each of them, and tell her why. Then, I want you to prepare letters to each person who donated time, talent, or money, for them to have for tax purposes.

"Okay. Is there anything else?"

Andy was thoughtful. "Make a note somewhere that if any of those nine musicians ever need hospitalization, and if they get their care here, the hospitalization costs will be complimentary. I will tell each of them that, but it needs to be a matter of record. Send a note out to the board members to that effect."

"Okay."

Andy went into his office and closed the door. He knelt down and prayed softly. "Lord, it was kind of hard last evening, explaining to Mike and Debbie what happened at the zoo yesterday. Thank you for guiding us. Thank you also for being with the Board at this meeting. You do everything exceedingly well, Lord." Thinking Janet might overhear him, Andy continued to pray silently.

When his phone rang about five minutes later, he quickly got up and touched the intercom button. "Yes, Janet?"

"Paul McMasters is on line two, Andy."

"Thank you." He punched a button. "Good afternoon, Pastor Paul! This is a pleasant surprise. What can I do for you?"

"I intended to talk to you on Sunday, but you left

67

rather quickly. After you, Abby, and the kids got home from the concert, I imagine you needed to take a nap!"

Andy laughed. "Actually, our neighbors from across the street assumed that we would need a break, so they brought their kids over to play with our kids in the basement. Abby and I both slept for a couple of hours."

"That's good. My wife and I had balcony seats, and we thoroughly enjoyed every moment." He paused. "Andy, I'm calling not only to express our appreciation for the concert, but to ask you to do something. I want you to lead a prayer team at the church."

"You want a prayer team? What would I do, or, rather, what would we do?"

"I'm going to ask ten people, including you, to be the initial members on the prayer team for three months. To start, you can share with the others what you learned from your Dad about prayer. You can also share as much as you want regarding your own prayer life. I'm hoping that our church will eventually become a truly prayer-centered church. Meanwhile, I'm asking you for a one-year commitment. Eleven months from now, you can tell me either you have had enough, or that you want to continue. Will you do this?"

Andy was thoughtful. "Let me pray about it, Paul."

"Okay. Can you let me know later this week, before Sunday?"

"Yes, of course, I can do that."

"Good! I'll talk to you later in the week. Bye!"

"Good-bye, Paul." The connection ended, and Andy hung up while staring out the window at nothing in particular.

+ + +

The rest of the day passed quickly. Coming in the front door of his house that evening, Andy's nose was

68

greeted with familiar aromas coming from the kitchen. Abby was sitting on the sofa watching the news on television, while the kids were playing on the floor. Andy took off his coat. "Hi Abby! Hi Kids!" The kids ran up and hugged his legs.

Abby smiled and waved. "Hi, handsome! Dinner won't be ready for about another half hour. How'd the board meeting go?"

Andy sat down beside her and gave her a quick kiss. "Everything went as expected. We can thank the Donovans again at Bible study, and I'm having Janet put in personal calls to the other seven."

"Good. What's this about?" She pointed toward the television and picked up the remote to turn up the volume.

".... Wendy Blackledge has our report from Anaheim. Wendy?

"Bob, I'm here at the front gate to Disneyland with its annual celebration of 'Gay Days.' It's this year's final day of the celebration, and several gay pride leaders made a point of telling those of us in the media how much they despise Christians, and how much they say Christians hate gays and lesbians. Some of the leaders said they could not understand Christian intolerance, some expressed hatred of anyone associated with Christianity, and a few had language even stronger."

"Thank you, Wendy. Wendy Blackledge, reporting from Disneyland. We are posting videos of those statements on our website. We turn now to a report from Amy Zorza, who's in Burbank with someone from Disney Parks and Resorts."

"Bob, I'm here with Cindy Smith, who used to

work for Disney Parks and Resorts. Cindy, what can you tell us about Gay Days at Disneyland?"

"I used to help plan Gay Days, but I'm no longer with Disney because I decided I wanted to be more active in defending gay and lesbian issues. I don't have anything against Disney or what happened today, but I can't say I represent them exactly either."

"Have you seen the video segments attacking Christians and their faith?"

"Yes, and I didn't hear anything new or surprising. I'm sure that bigoted Christians will object to what was said today, but we have our right to free speech in this country, don't we?"

"Thank you, Cindy. Back to you, Bob, in the studio."

Thank you, Amy. We'll be right back."

Andy hit the mute button. "There're a lot of things people do in this world that I don't approve of, but that doesn't mean I hate the people who do them. I hate adultery for the way it destroys families, but I don't hate all adulterers. I hated the theft of my grandfather's watch when I was living in a dorm in college, but I don't hate the thief. The rhetoric is so divisive."

Abby nodded. "I agree. I'm glad all of that nasty rhetoric was put on the web site instead of broadcasting it over the air. I'd not want our kids to hear it at their age." She got up. "I'm going to fix a salad. Do you want to get a shower before dinner?"

"Is that a hint?" He winked.

"No, of course not!" She leaned down, and they kissed briefly again.

"I think I'll feel more like eating if I do get a shower, though." As Andy got up from the sofa, he headed towards the bathroom, while Abby headed towards the kitchen.

Abby was a good cook. That evening they had slow roasted sliced beef with red potatoes and green beans. By the time the kids were bathed and in bed, both Andy and Abby were exhausted. They started watching an old movie with Peter O'Toole called "Creator," but both dozed off from exhaustion before it ended.

As the closing credits were rolling, they got up. Abby was sleepy. "If you shut everything down, I'll go check on the kids. Then we can head to bed."

"You have a deal." Andy turned off the TV and began moving about in their house, turning off the lights. After taking care of their nightly ablutions and getting ready for bed, they prayed aloud, kneeling at the foot of their bed, before calling it a night.

The next morning, Andy was in his office, reading the previous day's minutes of the board meeting, when his phone buzzed. He pushed a button. "Yes, Janet?"

"Steve Sudengae from the Press-Telegram is on line one."

"Okay." He pushed the button. "Good morning, this is Andy Hickman, how can I help you?"

"This is Steve Sudengae from the Press-Telegram. I understand that the hospital will be breaking ground for the new parking garage today. Is there going to be any kind of ceremony?"

Andy scratched his head. "To tell the truth, Steve, I talked to the architect about it last week, but he never got back to me."

"If there is going to be a ceremony, we'd like to cover it."

"I'll tell you what, I'll call him, and if we're going to have a ceremony, I'll have Janet, my secretary, call you.

Okay?"

"Great! Will I hear from her before noon?"

"I hope I'll get Tom in the next hour. I'll have Janet call you back as soon as we have a definite yes or no."

"Okay. Until then." The connection ended.

Andy hit the intercom button. "Janet, get Tom Elliott on the phone and ask him if he wants to break ground officially today. If so, let Steve Sudengae from the Press–Telegram know, and call Bill Sams at KNXT and let him know. Tell him if he can have a crew there to make a video segment, it would be fine. We owe him a lot for his past support of the project."

"Okay."

Andy leaned back in his chair and closed his eyes.

"Tom Elliott on line two, Andy."

He opened his eyes and reached for the phone. "Good morning, Tom."

"Good morning. I'm sorry I didn't get back to you. We do have a couple of hours to work with. How about I call a few TV stations and have the police cordon off some parking for the noon hour? I've got a gold-gilded shovel I've used at other ground breaking ceremonies."

"Great! I'll be there at 11:45. How's that?"

"Perfect! See you then!" The architect hung up.

"Janet, did you get all that?"

"Absolutely! I figured you'd want it."

"Thanks! You know me so well! Call Steve at the Newspaper and Bill at KNXT. After you do that, see if you can get me either Richard or Char Donovan."

"Right."

Once more, Andy leaned back and closed his eyes. Fifteen minutes later, Janet buzzed him. "Richard Donovan on line one, Andy."

He picked up the phone. "Good morning, Richard! I

hope I'm not disturbing you."

"Not really. Char and I are taking it easy today, catching up on phone calls and paperwork. What's up?"

"This is kind of last minute notice, but today at noon we're going to have a brief ground breaking ceremony on Elm Street at the site of the new parking garage. If either you or Char – or both of you – would like to be there, the newspaper and a few TV stations will cover it. You don't have to say anything if you don't want to, but if either of you would like to speak on behalf of the musicians who have paid for the project with that concert, that would be great."

"Hang on a minute, I'll tell Char." There were muffled sounds for about three minutes. "Okay, Andy, we'll both be there. By the way, did you hear about the controversy that started at Disneyland yesterday?"

"Yeah, we didn't see the speeches, but we heard about it on the news before dinner last night. Why?"

"We have a friend who works at the Disneyland Hotel. He said that a few dozen people checked out unexpectedly early this morning, and there was no line when the park opened."

"Is that unusual?"

"At this time of year? I'll say!"

"That's interesting. Last night, we tried watching a DVD of that old Peter O'Toole movie, "Creator," but we fell asleep before it ended. When we prayed before going to bed, we talked to the Lord quite a bit about what happened at Disneyland."

"I'm not surprised, knowing you two. By the way, Angel Madison and Lori Simpson from the seven are in town to do a private performance at the Petroleum Club here in Long Beach. If you like, I'll see if I can get them to join us at noon. What do you think?"

73

"That sounds great. I'll be there at about 11:45. I'll see you later."

"Right, see you later. Bye."

The rest of the morning went quickly. At 11:30, Andy went out the front door of the hospital, walked up to Elm Street, and over to the construction site. There appeared to be at least a dozen vans from the media there. He stayed on the opposite side of the street until he was directly across from an area cordoned off by yellow tape, and then he quickly traversed the street.

Tom Elliott was there with a gold-plated shovel. "Good morning, Andy. I've met your friends over there and got a few autographs. I was there Saturday night."

Andy smiled. "Good. Is this the shovel you told me about?"

Tom chuckled. "Right, this is it. Each time I use it, I have to have the shovel blade's thin gold plating re-done because it is scratched so easily. I have had some soil over there," he pointed, "already loosened up by other shovels, so nobody has to work too hard."

"That's fine, Tom. Let's tell the media, so that those who want to can broadcast this live."

Tom looked at his watch. "That'll be in about four minutes."

Andy turned and walked over to the yellow tape and those from the media behind it. "We'll start the ceremony at two minutes past twelve, about four minutes from now. Joining us today are Richard and Char Donovan, from the benefit concert on Saturday, along with Angel Madison and Lori Simpson from the Magnificent Seven. The man in the hard hat is Tom Elliott, the architect for the garage." He stopped and smiled. "The woman in the red dress is my beautiful wife, Abby. There are also three members of the

74

hospital's Board of Directors here, and they can introduce themselves if they choose to." Andy looked at his watch, turned, and went back to join Tom Elliott. He motioned for the musicians to join them.

Tom looked at Andy. "Are we ready? You can lead off."

Andy looked around. "Okay." He spoke louder. "Ladies and gentlemen, my name is Andy Hickman. I'm the administrator of Seaside Hospital. It is my pleasure to initiate this groundbreaking ceremony for the hospital's new parking garage. In our local newspaper, the Long Beach Independent Press–Telegram, Dandy Cooper was often described as an eccentric, and I'm told that Mr. Cooper enjoyed that reputation. For many years, quite a number of people saw Mr. Cooper's house as Long Beach's own authentic haunted house. Mr. Cooper also owned the lots both north and south of that house. Now, as everyone can see, all of that has been cleared away."

Andy paused and put his hand on Tom's shoulder. "This is Tom Elliott, the architect of this garage, who will answer any questions about the structure and its connecting tunnel after the groundbreaking ceremony." He looked to his left. "On my left are four of the musicians from Saturday's benefit concert. They are Char Donovan, Richard Donovan, Angel Madison, and Lori Simpson. Angel and Lori will be doing a private concert at the Petroleum Club tomorrow evening, and Richard will be performing with the Los Angeles Philharmonic on Friday and Saturday evening." There was scattered applause.

"The proceeds from ticket sales from the concert in the Long Beach Arena on Saturday are paying for 98.2% of the cost of construction." There was more applause.

"Richard, do you or any of the others want to say anything?" Richard shook his head. "Okay, let's do it."

Tom handed Andy the shovel, and Andy called Char, Lori, and Angel over. Each of them pushed the shovel into the ground and tossed some dirt forward. Richard followed suit, and then Andy. He turned to face the media and looked at all the guests. "Thank you, everyone, for coming today. This concludes our little ceremony."

The yellow barrier tapes came down, and media representatives came forward to ask questions. Richard approached Andy with Char. "We decided not to say anything because we had our time on stage on Saturday. This is the hospital's day."

Andy nodded, as Abby came forward and put her arm around him. He looked at Richard, Char, and their friends. "Thank you, thank you all again for your generous musical contributions on Saturday. The cheapest seats were sold for ten dollars, and the most expensive were five hundred each. Five corporate sponsors bought all the most expensive seats, paid several times what the tickets were worth, and then gave the seats away. It was sold out, and I think that it broke the record for a single event's receipts."

Lori Simpson smiled. "All of us were talking about it yesterday. It was great getting the nine of us together again for a reunion. The only thing that didn't happen was that Richard didn't do a classical piece."

Richard smiled and shook his head. "That's true, Lori, but this wasn't the place for it." He turned to Andy. "Whoever ran the soundboard did a great job. He or she should get a bonus!"

Richard took Andy's arm and took him to one side, away from the others. "Do you remember our conversation earlier about controversial things happening related to Disneyland?"

Richard nodded. "My friend at the hotel says that some people staying there take the monorail to the hotel for a better lunch than they can get in the park itself. He overheard some of them saying that the park seems not crowded at all. They didn't have to stand in line for any of the rides."

Andy nodded. "I wonder if there will be any follow-up in the news this evening."

"It's hard to say. I know a spokesperson for Blue Whale Online Retail said something about the free speech rights of the LGBT community, saying if someone wanted to be vocal about despicable Christians, they had a perfect right to express their hatred."

"Really? It's hard to imagine the world's largest online retailer making a statement like that."

Richard nodded. "Char and I watch both CNN and Fox News, and for local news, we watch either KCBS or KTTV. The controversy still seems to be simmering." He paused. "Will you and Abby be coming for Bible study this evening?

Andy smiled. "Yeah, we plan to. We can talk more about this later."

"Right. I see someone who wants my attention. I've got to go." Richard walked over to a journalist with a microphone and camera crew. "Good afternoon!"

"Mr. Donovan, I'm Connie Epson from CBS News. Will you and your wife, Charlotte, be doing any more concerts with The Magnificent Seven soon?"

Richard smiled. "We enjoy playing together, but we also have our separate careers. We are talking about getting together once a year to do benefits like the one we just did at Long Beach's Convention Center. Our next benefit will be for Samaritan's Purse, but the date and location are not yet firm."

"When you and your wife first became famous, you became known because you cast lots to determine God's will, and you had determined time of the Yellowstone eruption before it occurred. Do you and your wife still cast lots to determine God's will?"

Richard nodded. "We cast lots every week, but only when we feel inspired to do so. We pray every day, but we do not always cast lots."

"Did this last benefit concert happen because of casting lots?"

"It was a factor." Richard paused. "Excuse me, but my wife and I have to get back to our practicing for our next performance together."

"But Mr. Donovan...."

7.
Two Events, One Day

The phone rang, and Char put down the sponge and dried her hands. She picked up the handset from the phone on the kitchen wall. "Hello?"

"Good morning, Char, this is Abby."

"Good morning! How are you?"

"I'm fine. Being Saturday, the kids are home, and I'm toying with possibilities. Are you and Richard doing anything today?"

"Richard's in London, remember? He's performing with the London Philharmonic this week. He'll be back late tomorrow night or early Monday morning. I was thinking about taking the kids to the mall. I figure they can start telling me what they want for Christmas."

"Really? I was thinking about going out today too, because Andy has to work. It wasn't much, and he was going to put it off until Monday, but then he got a call a little while ago. Something strange was happening in the emergency ward, and he was called in because a patient insisted on seeing the hospital's administrator."

"So, shall we do something together? Do you want to bring your kids and join me and mine at the mall?"

"We could do that, but Toby has been pestering me for weeks to go to Knott's Berry Farm."

"Really? Richard and I haven't been there since we've been married. After Walter and Cordelia Knott died, and the family was bought out by Cedar Fair Entertainment, Richard and I saw that there were quite a few changes. I assume there have been a lot more changes since then. I'd like to see it again, and I'm sure the kids will enjoy it. I can put in a voice mail to Richard about what we're doing."

"Great! I'll do the same for Andy. Where shall we meet?"

"Why don't you and the kids come up the hill here? My SUV is big enough for all of us, and I can arrange for VIP gate passes. Cedar Fair Entertainment owns the place, and they have wanted to talk to Richard and me about doing a gig for them. I'll let them present what they're proposing over lunch, and Cedar Fair will write our expenses off as a business expense. Everyone wins that way. I can just call and have Bobbi, our manager, arrange it. I'll see you when you get here, okay?"

"Great! See you later!" The connection ended.

Char hung up and punched a number she knew just as well as Abby's. "Good morning, Bobbi, this is Char Donovan."

"Good morning Char. You hardly ever call on a weekend. What's up?"

"Two weeks ago, you told me about how Cedar Fair Entertainment wants Richard and me to do another gig with the 'Magnificent Seven,' this time with their sponsorship. When we get together as the larger group, we want to always do the gigs as benefits. I don't know if Cedar Fair Entertainment has that in mind or not, but it is not negotiable."

"Lori Simpson told me that the other day when we made tentative plans for a benefit concert for Samaritan's Purse."

"That's good. My friend Abby Hickman and I are going to Knott's Berry Farm today with our kids. I can give someone fifteen minutes to present Cedar Fair's ideas to me after lunch."

"Okay, it will be just you because Richard's in London at the moment, right?"

"Right. My friend and our kids will be there, but that should not be a problem. Whoever makes the presentation won't dare to get too fancy or the kids will get restless."

Bobbi laughed. "I think I'll tell them that you want a presentation in writing, and that they can discuss it with you very, very briefly over lunch."

Char smiled, as Bobbi knew her so well. "Perfect. Call me back as soon as you have it set up."

"Okay, bye!" She hung up.

Char called out, "Kids! Come to the kitchen for a moment!" She heard them giggling before they ran into the kitchen. "We're going to Knott's Berry Farm today with Abby and her kids."

"Yea!" They turned around to run out.

Char said, "Hold it!" They stopped. "We'll leave as soon as Abby and her kids get here. We're going in our SUV, so go to the garage and get the trash out of there, and make sure it is clean. We'll leave in less than an hour."

"Okay!" The kids ran off.

+ + +

Being the weekend, there were fewer cars on the streets, so Andy could park across the street from a side entrance to the Hospital. Turning off his car's engine, he looked in the rear-view mirror as he tightened his tie.

Andy usually didn't wear a suit on Saturdays, and he was puzzled as to why he had been asked to come in. Walking briskly, Andy went across the street into the hospital and strode down the hall to the emergency waiting area. As he went in, he saw a familiar nurse stand up with a tall gentleman in a suit. "Good morning, Julie."

A recent graduate of the Harris College of Nursing at TCU, she was extremely competent as an ER nurse. "Good morning sir, this is Tom Moore. He represents Halle Beebee, the faith healer. Mr. Moore, this is Andrew Hickman, our hospital's administrator."

"Good morning. What is going on?"

Andy shook the man's hand. Tom Moore oozed confidence in a slick way. "Good morning, it's good to meet you, Mr. Hickman. Can we sit down and talk quietly?"

"Certainly." Nodding slightly to a security guard standing nearby, Andy led Tom Moore over to a corner of the waiting room. They pulled up chairs to face each other. Some other people nearby tried to come closer, but the guard held them back.

Andy looked at the man squarely. "Why did you need to see me, Mr. Moore?"

Tom Moore glanced around the room at the others and spoke in almost a whisper. "My client was getting ready to do his evening presentation when he was suddenly very ill. He told me to tell the gathering audience that today's presentation was canceled due to an emergency at Seaside Hospital, and that he had agreed to come here. That's what I did, but somehow the media have decided that my client is ill. First of all, I want to be sure that my client's privacy is intact."

Andy nodded. "All hospital admissions are confidential. We will not make statements to the media without the consent of the patient or his legal representative."

The agent nodded. "I understand that. I am wondering if you could make an announcement to the

82

effect that Halle Beebee is visiting patients in ICU and praying with them."

Andy shook his head. "No. I will never lie to the media, and the hospital is not going to do publicity for your client."

The agent seemed truly shocked. "Oh, no, you misunderstand. I simply want my Mr. Beebee to pray with patients openly, while he is here."

Andy shook his head and turned to the nurse. "Julie?" She came over closer. Speaking quietly, he asked, "Has Mr. Beebee been admitted?" Julie nodded. "Thank you, you can return to your station." Andy turned back to the agent. "Listen to me carefully. First, do you have a medical power of attorney with your client? I need to see it in writing."

The man blinked and shook his head. "I've sent for his brother."

"Very well. Since you are not family, you won't be allowed back into the patient area until we access what is happening with your client, and his doctor gives permission for visitors."

"What? I'm his agent! I've every right!"

Andy shook his head. "Not once he is admitted to this hospital, you don't." He looked up to see Julie beaconing to him. "Mr. Moore, I'm going back into the patient area. Someone will come out and let you know how things are going when occasion warrants." He stood up. "I repeat, someone will let you know when we know."

Andy walked briskly towards Julie and on into the emergency care area. Dr. John Cochran was standing at the nurses' station, looking at a chart, and he glanced up as Andy approached. "Hey, Andy. I'm sorry you had to come in on a Saturday. I've got a celebrity as a patient."

"You've got Halle Beebee as your patient?"

John nodded. "I'm on duty for another couple of ours. After he signed his admission paperwork, he wanted to head to ICU to pray with patients there. I told him that he was our patient now, and, as his doctor, I had plenty of tests to run on him before he had any time to do things he wanted to do. He protested, but I told him he could either do things my way or check out. He said he wanted to see someone that outranks me."

Andy grinned. "His agent tried to manipulate me out in the waiting room. Be on the lookout for a tall guy in his forties named Tom Moore. Mr. Moore admitted that he did not have medical power of attorney and that Mr. Beebee's brother has been called."

John nodded. "I talked to Richard Beebee, my patient's brother, about fifteen minutes ago. He'll be here in about an hour. If you want, why don't you talk to the patient? His testing will start in less than ten minutes."

Andy nodded. "What bed is he in?"

"Eight."

The two of them walked towards the screened area. John made the introduction. "Mr. Beebee, you asked to speak to someone who outranks me here at the hospital. This is Andy Hickman, the Administrator of Seaside Hospital."

Halle Beebee raised his hand weakly to shake. "Mr. Hickman, it is good to meet you. Dr. Cochran, would you please leave us alone for a few moments?" John nodded and stepped out. The patient spoke quietly. "Mr. Hickman, are you a religious man?"

Andy nodded. "I try to be faithful to Jesus. Why do you ask?"

"Most of my adult life I've been healing people. I'd like to think that .... No, Mr. Hickman, I won't go there.

84

I'm known as a healer, I've built a sizable reputation as someone who provides others with healing, and now I find myself in a hospital, probably needing healing."

Andy nodded. "Go on."

"It's embarrassing! I've never been sick. As a child, I didn't catch anything, not even colds or the flu. You can ask my brother when he gets here."

"Did you think that if you ever got sick you would heal yourself?"

"It never occurred to me that I would ever get sick!"

Andy was thoughtful. "You asked me a moment ago if I was religious. Are you religious? Do you pray?"

"Sure, I pray with people when I'm asked. I know how to pray."

Andy shook his head. "That's not what I'm asking. I'm simply asking if, for you, is prayer a lifeline, or is it a lifestyle?"

He stared at Andy. "Are you some kind of lay preacher?"

He shook his head. "My dad was a pastor, but I'm simply a hospital administrator. I've recently been asked to lead a prayer team at my church."

Halle Beebee looked down. "I guess God uses me to heal sometimes, and when it happens, I make the most of it, but it is inconsistent. I .... You asked me if prayer was a lifeline or a lifestyle, and I guess for me, it is a lifeline that I throw out, mostly for others."

Julie came and stood at the entrance. "Excuse me. Mr. Beebee, an orderly will be with you in a moment to take you to diagnostic imaging, okay?"

"Okay." He looked over at Andy. "Mr. Hickman, thank you for your time. I hope you'll keep what I said confidential."

Andy nodded and stood up. "Yes, sir, I'll do that. It

was nice meeting you." Andy went out and back to the waiting room. Tom Moore stood up as Andy approached. "Mr. Moore, some tests are being run. If you're hungry, we have a pretty good cafeteria. Just go down that hall," he pointed, "and follow the signs."

"Thank you, I could use a bite to eat."

Andy turned and went to a small multipurpose meeting room. Picking up a phone, he punched the number for his voice mail. There was one message.

"Andy, Char and I are taking our kids to Knott's Berry Farm. We should be back sometime after lunch. Maybe the next time we go, Richard will be in town, and we can make it a bigger event with our whole families and a longer day. I love you."

+ + +

It was a beautiful day for visiting Knott's Berry Farm. After walking awhile, they stopped to watch the Silver Bullet roller coaster. Richie began begging his Mom to let him ride it. Char shook her head. "None of you are big enough yet to ride this, or any of the roller coasters."

Abby smiled. "I think that if both our families come back before the kids can ride, I think they can watch as their parents try some of the coasters."

Char nodded and laughed. "I agree!"

For almost two hours, they explored other parts of the park, and they all rode some of the smaller rides. It was just before noon when they went into Mrs. Knott's Chicken Dinner Restaurant. Char and Richard's manager, Bobbi, had arranged for a small private dining room for them. They were quickly ushered inside.

They sat down around a large table. A moment later, a tall woman in an impeccably tailored suit entered. She had cascades of flaming red hair falling on her shoulders, and her blue eyes seemed to shine as she smiled and introduced herself. "Hello! I'm Sandra Jo Maffett from Cedar Fair Entertainment."

Char nodded and shook her hand. "I'm Char Donovan, and this is my dear friend, Abby Hickman. Kids, say hello to Ms. Maffett."

"Hi, Ms. Maffett," the kids said almost together. The woman sat down.

A server appeared with a tray with tumblers of water. Char thanked her for her glass and spoke. "Let's go ahead and order lunch first, and we can talk while we're eating. Sandra Jo, I assume you have a written proposal for me."

She nodded. "Call me Sandra. Yes, I can give it to you after lunch."

After the server took their orders, Sandra decided to make casual conversation. "Our attendance here at Knott's Berry Farm has gone up about five percent in the last few weeks. We've hired a few more people."

Abby nodded. "It's pretty crowded out there, but it's not unexpected. Did the increase come after Disneyland's Gay Days celebration?"

Sandra grinned. "We don't talk much about the competition." The other women laughed. "Seriously, we had a slight bump when the competition's celebration began, but we've had still another bump since then."

Char nodded. "That's interesting to know. Richard and I pray about just about everything we do. It's public knowledge that we cast lots when making decisions."

Sandra smiled. "I've read some interesting material on you and Richard in preparation for this meeting. I understand that you began to deal with our federal government during your honeymoon."

Char laughed. "It began just as we got back from

our honeymoon in Europe, yes. In hindsight that looks and sounds more than a little weird, but the eruption of Mount Yellowstone created strange situations for many people. From the very beginning, our being devout Christians has been public knowledge. Sometimes we find that people will be choosing their words carefully not to offend us, but neither of us takes offense easily. We don't allow ourselves to be victims."

Sandra nodded. "Speaking of choosing words carefully, do either of you remember how several days ago a spokesperson for Blue Whale Online Retail made a statement in support of free speech for those in the LGBT community?"

Abby nodded. "As I recall, she, in essence, said that their hatred of Christians was understandable."

"That's pretty close. Her name is Brooke Vargas. I knew her in my undergraduate days at the University of Pennsylvania. She sent out an email to friends early this morning, saying that she had been transferred to Cairo, Egypt. I emailed her back, asking if this was something she had wanted. She answered no, but after her casual remarks about free speech, Blue Whale Retail's online sales dropped several percentage points over the subsequent 48 hours, and then things leveled out at a lower rate. The company sent an email to all its customers regarding free speech for everyone, and went on to say that hate speech is never appropriate. Their sales bumped up half a percentage point or so, but her transfer was punitive and went through."

Char's mouth hung open a moment. "Wow! That's an almost unbelievable corporate response from Blue Whale."

Two servers came in with their food, and as the kids began to eat ravenously, the adults talked about another concert featuring the Donovans with the Magnificent Seven.

+ + +

Andy finished his lunch in the hospital's cafeteria. As he was enjoying a second cup of coffee, his pager went off. Taking out his cell phone, he dialed the hospital's operator. "This is Andy Hickman. I was just paged."

"Yes. The patient in 6011 wants to speak with you. He says he talked with you earlier in the emergency ward."

"I see. Thank you." For a moment, he looked out the window into an atrium, and then he slowly closed his eyes. A few minutes later, he took his tray to a self-serve window, walked out of the cafeteria, and walked to the nearest elevator.

When Andy knocked on the door of room 6011, he heard a voice call out to come in. Beside the bed stood John Cochran and a tall, slightly overweight man whose features were similar to those of the patient. Doctor Cochran gestured. "Andy, this is Richard Beebee, our patient's brother. Richard, this is Andy Hickman, our hospital's administrator."

Andy shook his hand. "Hello. I understand you have your brother's medical power of attorney. It is up to you as to what information is given out to Tom Moore or anyone else."

The man nodded. "I understand." He paused. "Tom can be a real pain in the butt, but he's basically a good guy."

Halle Beebee spoke softly. "I called you, Mr. Hickman, because after I told my brother about my previous conversation with you, he suggested we talk and maybe pray together."

John Cochran hung his stethoscope around his neck. "Andy, Mr. Beebee told me that you asked him if prayer for him was a lifeline or a lifestyle. I told him I know you well enough to say you're willing to talk about prayer, and that you don't press religion on anyone unless you're pressured with questions. I'll leave the three of you alone to talk. I've got other patients to see." He nodded at Andy, and he strode out.

The famous healer smiled weakly. "I told Richard that in all my conversations with pastors through the years, none of them had ever asked me that question."

Richard nodded. "I must admit, it has given me pause as well." He looked at his brother. "How much shall I tell him?"

The patient blinked. "No secrets here, Richard."

He nodded and turned to Andy. "I'm two years older than my brother. When we were children, we went to church services every Sunday, and sometimes the pastor or the elders prayed for those who were sick. A few times, they did a laying on of hands for someone when it was requested. Praying became almost a game for us, and we prayed for anything and everything. I am not at all sure our two cats and our dog ever got used to us holding them down so we could pray for them."

Andy chuckled. "Did your church's pastor know about all this?"

Richard nodded. "We learned as adults that the pastor assured our mother that we would grow tired of it and stop eventually. When I started to pay attention to girls, I lost interest in healing prayer, but Richard continued. When one of our cats, Nicky, was killed by a passing car in front of our house, our Dad wrapped her in a towel and took her to the back yard to bury her. Richard insisted on praying, so Dad stopped while he put his hand on the towel and cried out an impassioned prayer. While he was praying, Nicky crawled out of the towel and ran off."

Andy raised his eyebrows. "Really?"

They both nodded, and Richard continued. "Neither of us tells that story very often." Andy nodded. "Mr. Hickman, do you consider prayer to be a lifestyle for yourself?"

Andy nodded. "May I share something from a sermon I heard my Dad preach when I was a teenager?" They both nodded. "Dad said that if we consider all Christians around the world, regardless of church affiliation or background, the people that call themselves Christians fall into one of three categories - followers, fans, and wannabes." The two other men looked at him intently. "Wannabes are primarily Christians in name only. They engage in few, if any, of the practices that most people associate with Christianity."

Richard nodded. "It seems as though that can be the 'default religion' for many I know, but they never go to church."

Andy smiled. "Right. Fans are those who, like the wannabes, call themselves Christians, but they also engage in at least some of the practices of being a Christian, such as public worship, tithing, private worship, Bible study, or perhaps one or more of a dozen or so other disciplines. If there is a conflict, however, between what they want to do and what they think God may want them to do, they do what they feel like doing or what they think is right."

The healer cocked his head. "Can you give us an example?"

Andy nodded. "Sure. There are families that go to

church every Sunday until school soccer practice begins with Sunday morning practices. Instead of finding another time when they can engage in public worship as a family, they don't even set aside time for private family worship. Instead, they abandon worship altogether until soccer season is over."

The two brothers were silent. The younger one closed his eyes a moment, then he opened them, and he spoke softly, saying, "This morning you said you try to be faithful to Jesus. Do you fall into the third category?"

Andy nodded, "I try to be a follower. Followers do their best to make God their top priority in everything. When I got your page a while ago, I was in the cafeteria. I simply closed my eyes and talked to Jesus about your call before coming up here."

Richard looked at Andy. "How do I pray for a brother who has inoperable cancer?"

Andy glanced back and forth at the two of them. "God knows everything, so there's nothing we can tell Him that He does not already know. I don't think that the particular words that we use are what matter. I only know from experience that God is ready to use us if we are willing to surrender to His will. We have to embrace God and His response to our prayers, no matter what. My Dad would ask permission to put his hand on a person's shoulder or on their head while he prayed. As he did so, he could imagine God's spirit coming upon him and flowing onto and through the person for whom he was praying. I have had similar experiences."

Halle looked at him. "Does that work?"

"I'm not sure that it matters in the least whether I am convinced it works, but I do it anyway."

"Will you pray for me before you go?"

"Sure. Richard, put your right hand on Halle's head

and give me your other hand. Halle, I'm going to put my left hand on your shoulder, okay?" Halle nodded. "Most of my prayer will be silent. I'll conclude simply by saying amen." The two brothers nodded, and Andy closed his eyes. "Father, you've brought the three of us together as men of faith. We surrender to your will and ask that you use us for your glory." For several minutes, none of the men moved. Then Andy said, "Amen."

Halle looked up at him. "Thank you, sir. I guess we'll know God's answer soon enough, won't we?"

Andy nodded. "God's timing is always perfect because He is eternal. It's been good meeting you, Richard. I'll leave the two of you to continue visiting." Andy turned and went out.

+ + +

Across the street from Andy's mother's home, children were playing in the park. As Trina watched through her living room window, she remembered the time when she and Huck took Andy, Linda, and Bill to the park, and one of the children fell off the merry-go-round and hit his head.

> On the ground, the boy did not move as his mother rushed over to him. "Steve! Wake up, Steve!"

> Huck and Trina were soon by her side, and the mother looked at Huck. "Aren't you the pastor of the big church on Ximeno Avenue?"

> Huck nodded. "Yes. You're Tonia Adams, aren't you?"

> She nodded. "Yes."

> "Would you like me to pray for you and your son?"

> "Oh please, yes, do that!"

"Most of my prayer will be silent." Huck put one hand on little Steve's face and took his mother's hand in his other hand. "Master, I lift up Steve Adams and his mother to you in prayer. They hunger for you at this moment, and they need you." Huck was silent for about a minute. "In Jesus' precious and powerful name, I pray, Amen."

Remembering that incident, Trina prayed. "Lord, I remember that so vividly. When they checked out Steve at the hospital, he was fine. He's now an art teacher at Jordan High School. I wish I could have heard some of Huck's silent prayers, Lord. Don't I wish?! I sure could have learned a lot."

8.
A Vacation and a Miracle

Andy and Abby needed to get away for a few days. Trina offered to help Abby's parents take care of the grand kids for a few days while their kids got time off.

In their room at Yosemite Lodge at the Falls, Abby put the newspaper she was holding down onto her lap. "I'm so used to Long Beach's *Press-Telegram.* It is very different to read this *Fresno Bee*, but I kind of like it." She paused to read some more, and then she looked up again. "I miss the kids, but I'm glad my parents were willing to take the kids for a few days while we come up here. Trina did not need to offer to help in order to convince them."

Andy nodded, "I always find being here in the Valley very peaceful, especially during the winter months like this. When there're no huge crowds around, it's like being in a rather cold spa for healing and rest."

Abby smiled. "It was fun to hike some of the trails at Happy Isles this afternoon. I'm glad that we decided to walk all the way back here instead of take the shuttle. I particularly like walking the Mirror Lake loop." She stopped to read another paragraph. "I miss the quiet thunder of Yosemite Falls, but then there're those loud crashes of the huge icicles once in a while. I like it here."

She was quiet several minutes as she continued to read the paper. Turning a page, she looked up. "Wasn't Halle Beebee a patient at the hospital a few months ago?"

Andy nodded. "Yes. I saw him twice, and I prayed with him and his brother the second time."

"Yeah, I vaguely remember. There's an article about him here in the paper. He has retired and is living off some investments. He and his wife now have a home near Jacob Lake, just north of the Grand Canyon."

"He got married?"

Abby nodded, "You'll have to read the article. It's really interesting. They met late last summer and decided to honeymoon on the North Rim of the Grand Canyon. They fell in love with the area and bought a home just north of the park."

Andy reached towards her and the paper she was holding. "Is the article in the first section?"

She shook her head, "No, here. It's in the second section." She handed it to him. "He's in Fresno for a conference on prayer at a large church there. He looks like he's in good health."

Andy began reading. After a few minutes, he looked up. "He was an interesting challenge for me. When he was admitted to the emergency ward, both he and his manager tried to take control of the situation. As with a few other celebrities we've dealt with, I diplomatically had to help him understand that unless he checked himself out the hospital, his doctor was in control. Judging from this article, it appears that he has fully regained his health."

Abby got up out of her chair, crossed the room, and opened the sliding glass door. A cold breeze came in as she stepped out on the balcony. From their second-floor room's vantage point, off to the right, she could see the ice-encrusted cliff comprising the first drop of Yosemite Falls. Below their balcony was a short path to the parking lot where their rental SUV was parked.

Shivering, she turned and went back inside. "It's really brisk out there!"

Andy grinned and nodded, and then he looked at his watch. "Are you hungry?" Abby nodded. "It's a little early for dinner, but if we start walking to the Food Court now we'll be at the beginning of the lines."

Abby smiled. "It must be the altitude, but I'm famished! At lunch, I had a bowl of that delicious vegetarian split pea soup and a salad, but I'll want more tomorrow at lunch. I think. Did I see chili there?"

"Yeah. I think tomorrow I'll get a burger but have it put on a plate instead of in a basket. Then I'll put chili over it."

"Oooh! That sounds good. Maybe I'll try that, and possibly I'll get some fruit too, but that's tomorrow. I don't want to go back to the Food Court for dinner. Do you want to splurge, go to the Ahwahnee Hotel dining room, and immerse ourselves in a gourmet dinner?" Andy cocked his head, thinking. She went on, "We could also go to the Mountain Room and get a steak, or we can head on out of the park to Yosemite View Lodge. We've had some great food out there too."

Andy smiled. "It seems to me, I remember Char and Richard telling us that the chef out at Yosemite View Lodge is a friend of theirs."

Abby nodded. "Char said that he had a specialty that's not always on the menu. Do you remember his name?"

Thoughtfully, he hesitated, and then his face brightened. "Jonathan Hu! That's his name! Let's go out there and ask if he's cooking tonight. If so, we can ask him what he recommends."

"Great!"

"Let's take our new camera. I want some newer

images since I sold a few through the Ansel Adams Gallery six months ago."

Abby smiled. "You're just a little boy again when you get out your camera here in the valley, aren't you?"

"Yep!" He grinned.

They put on their winter coats and hats, and a few minutes later they were downstairs. Soon, they were in their SUV headed west on Northside Drive. There were a few puffy snowflakes drifting down, but not enough snow to make driving difficult. Just before they got to the turnoff for Pohono Bridge, Andy pulled into the parking area for Valley View. There were no other cars.

Andy reached toward the back seat floor and retrieved a window pod. After fastening his camera to it, he rolled down his driver's side window enough to clamp the pod to the window. "I like the way the fog is drifting across the meadow, with that cloud wrapped around the Cathedral Peaks east of Bridalveil Fall, don't you?" He made some images.

"It's almost magical, isn't it?"

"Uh-huh." Andy dismounted the camera and window pod and put it behind his seat.

Abby reached around and put a lap robe over it. "I'm getting really hungry, Andy. Let's get on down the hill."

"Okay."

There was no traffic as they left the Pohono Bridge area, but Andy drove under the speed limit. "With this snow coming down, and as cold as it is, there might be black ice, so I'm taking it slowly."

Abby nodded. "Most of the road between here and El Portal is downhill, so you can shift down."

Andy nodded.

+ + +

It was almost three hours later, after eating a very large dinner, when Andy and Abby pulled out of the parking lot of Yosemite View Lodge. They headed east, back into the park. Abby was content. "I don't know that I've ever had a better meal in my life, Andy. I did not know that Rex Stout had published a Nero Wolfe cookbook. When Jonathan Hu said there was a chapter on cold-weather dinners, I had to try one. After all, we've both been Nero Wolfe fans since we were teenagers. I don't think I could eat or drink anything more until tomorrow!"

Andy nodded. "When he brought us that planked Porterhouse steak, two inches thick, with some juices in the plank's trough...."

Abby nodded. "I can still picture it when we first saw it!"

"It looked so beautiful with the parsley and slices of lime. The mashed potatoes were just right with the steak's juices - we didn't need gravy. That's for sure."

She smiled. "The other surprise was how those mushrooms were sliced so thick and slightly underdone. When we get home, I'm going to see if I can order that cookbook, even if I have to get a used copy."

Andy pulled to a stop at the entrance station, but they just passed on through because the rangers had closed up shop for the day. "When we get to the clearing near Cascade Falls, let's open the moon roof, and see if the clouds have cleared out. The skies are supposed to be clear tonight, and it's already pitch black out there this time of the year.""

They drove in silence for a while. Abby opened the moon roof and looked up. "It looks clear except for a few wisps." She closed the roof again. "It's cold out there!" She pressed a button on the dashboard a few times.

"It's 22 degrees!"

Andy had to veer to the right as they arrived at Pohono Bridge. "Since it's clear enough, let's turn right up here at the junction and go up to the Tunnel View parking lot. Why don't you mount the ultra-wide-angle lens on the camera?"

"Right." She reached behind his seat, and quickly she changed the lens. "This is a manual focus Zeiss lens, remember? I'm setting the lens wide open, and focused on infinity. How many seconds of exposure?"

"Make it ten seconds, and double-check to see that it is set up to bracket exposures with automatic ISO plus and minus two stops."

"Are we still shooting everything raw?"

Andy pulled into the tunnel parking lot. "Right. It will be fun in our spare time to play with the post processing of bracketed image sets in the months ahead. I also bracketed those images at Yosemite View earlier."

He parked in the lot with his window facing east. "I'll tip it up slightly, so that when I crop it to sixteen by nine we'll take out most of the foreground and get more of the stars." He quickly got the camera set up and focused. He turned off the engine and the lights. "Hold still."

As the camera followed its program, they looked at each other. Abby whispered. "I hope this comes out."

"I hope so too." They both sighed. "Let's do it again, but at five seconds." He turned the shutter's control dial. "Okay. Let's hold still again." In a few moments, they sighed again. Andy took the pod off the window and handed it to her. "Let's head down the hill."

Abby held the outfit in her lap. "When we get down there, let's pull just beyond Bridal Veil Fall and make some images of the stars above El Capitan. I can

100

probably get a good image set from my window of the fall."

After photographing the stars above the famous monolith and the adjacent fall, and after making similar images of Yosemite Falls with the stars above, it was just after ten. Both were getting sleepy. As they approached the chapel on their right, a car pulled out of the chapel's parking lot very rapidly. Andy slowed down as the other car sped quickly out of sight. "That's strange. I suppose they could have been praying, but what's that van doing in the back of the lot?" Andy pulled in and drove up close to the van.

As Andy put the SUV in park, Abby reached over, took Andy's hand, and closed her eyes. "Lord, you have us here for a reason. Please show us why."

Andy opened his eyes. "I don't like this, my love. I have a bad feeling about this."

"I do too. Let's go look."

Leaving the engine running, Andy got out, and as Abby came around the rear of the SUV, they joined hands again and walked towards the van. As they approached, they could hear a soft beeping sound coming from inside.

As he slid open the side door, they saw a large metal box with metal braces coming up from the floor, holding the box in place. There was a pink glow reflected off the ceiling. He shook his head. "This looks bad, very bad."

As Andy stepped in with his head down, Abby followed. As they looked over the top edge of the box, her eyes grew wide. "Is this a bomb? Dynamite? C4?"

"Yeah, it is a bomb, but...." He looked at it carefully. "Twenty-eight minutes and a few seconds, but... Uh-Oh."

"What?"

"In my training at Eglin Air Force Base in Florida, I only saw pictures of this. This is the real thing."

"What kind of real thing?"

"This is a thermonuclear device!" He paused. "There's no time to get a team here, let alone get the valley evacuated. It's up to us, Abby." He swallowed a dry swallow. We always pray in a crisis. Let's get out and pray."

"Wait!" Abby took out her cell phone. "I hope my phone works! Cell phone coverage here in the valley is spotty." She punched numbers. "I've got a connection. It's ringing."

"Who?"

"Richard and Char."

"Hello? Abby?"

"Char! Please forgive me for calling so late! I was expecting to get your answering service!"

"No, we had late calls to make. What's up?"

"I'm putting this on the speaker-phone. Get Richard and do the same."

"Right. Richard, it's Andy and Abby, with some kind of emergency."

The sound was different on their speaker phones. "What's up?" asked Richard.

Andy swallowed again. "Don't talk, just listen. Abby and I are at Yosemite Chapel, standing next to a van. Inside the van is a thermonuclear device, with a timer set to go off in just over twenty-five minutes. There's no time to get a bomb disposal team here, let alone evacuate the valley. My training was over ten years ago in Florida. We need to do more than just pray. Please cast lots for us. Maybe The Master will tell us what to do."

"Right! said Char. There was a pause. "Lord, will you

help us in this emergency?" ... Pause.

"Heads-heads-heads! Yes!" came Richard's voice. "Lord, should Andy try to disarm the bomb?" ... Pause.

Char spoke excitedly. "Tails-tails-tails! No! ... Master, should Abby try to disarm the bomb?" There was a pause.

"Tails-tails-tails!" Richard sounded disappointed. They paused. ""Father, should we just pray?" They paused again.

Char sounded incredulous. "Tails-tails-tails!"

There was a period of silence. Andy cleared his throat. "Are you still there?"

"Yes," said Richard. "Char's praying silently. Hold on."

Char's voice returned, very calm. "Master, should Andy simply command the bomb and van to be gone?"

Richard was excited again. "Heads-heads-heads!"

Abby was incredulous. "You have got to be kidding!"

Abby and Andy could not see Richard smiling and shaking his head. "It's simple, Abby, Andy. It's in Matthew's gospel. I think. Hang on, I've got my Bible." He paused as he turned pages. "Here it is. Jesus says, in Matthew 21:21 'Truly, I say to you, if you have faith and do not doubt, you will not only do what has been done to the fig tree, but even if you say to this mountain, 'Be taken up and thrown into the sea,' it will happen."

Suddenly, Andy was very calm. "Abby, assuming you're with me, we'll do this together. Hang on you two."

They got out of the van, and they walked around to stand in front of it. Abby turned and put the phone on a small boulder behind them. "Richard, Char, you will hear what we pray. We ask that you be in agreement with us, okay?"

The two voices in Long Beach spoke together.

"Okay."

Abby wrapped her arms around her husband. "Whatever you pray, Andy, I'm in full agreement with you."

Andy reached out, put his hands on the shallow hood of the van, and closed his eyes. "Heavenly Father, we're standing on your promises and, more specifically on the promise of your Son, Jesus, Our Savior. ... In the precious and powerful name of Jesus, your Son, and Our Savior, we command this van to be gone, leaving this Earth and its atmosphere. Alleluia! Amen!"

Andy and Abby stumbled backward as the van sailed into the sky with a blast of air. It was out of sight in less than a second. Together, they exclaimed. "Praise God!" They went to the cell phone on the boulder. "Char, Richard, are you there?"

"Yes!"

"The van is gone! It disappeared in less than a second!"

Richard spoke quietly. "I suppose both of you know that we can't talk about this except with each other, and privately, right?"

Andy nodded absentmindedly. "I understand what you're saying, Richard, but before we make a firm commitment, one way or the other, about anything, I think all four of us need to pray about it. When we are back in Long Beach next week, maybe we can get together, and you two can cast lots to see what The Master wants us to do."

Char's voice was strong. "I agree! Richard and I will pray about it, but we'll wait until you get here before we cast lots concerning this."

Andy nodded. "Good. Abby and I are going to go into the chapel now and pray. We'll see you two when we get

104

back home. Thank you for being with us in this. I don't think we'll ever forget this!"

Char was very enthusiastic. "Absolutely! You're welcome! Thanks for letting us be part of it!"

"I agree!" Richard's voice was stronger. "We'll see you two next week! Bye!"

"Bye!" As Andy and Abby spoke, the connection ended. Andy went over and shut off the engine of their SUV, and then they went into the chapel and prayed.

About twenty minutes later, Andy and Abby came down the chapel steps, and, shivering, walked quickly to the SUV. As Andy opened the door for Abby, a brilliant light lit up the sky for several seconds. Then it was pitch dark again. They looked at each other and nodded. Andy was solemn. "The bomb still had to go off."

Driving back from the chapel to Yosemite Lodge, they were both quiet except for the rush of air through the SUV's heating system. Andy found a parking space only a few yards from the stairs leading up to the second floor of their building and their room.

By the time they had locked their door, taken a shower, turned off the light, and snuggled up together, it was well after midnight. They slept soundly.

The next morning, after praying and reading the Bible, Andy asked, "We've got reservations for two nights in the ski shelter at Glacier Point starting this evening. Are you up for it?"

"Am I? After what God did last night, I'm willing to tackle anything! How soon do we catch the bus?"

"We have to get the first bus, which is less than an hour from now. We have enough time to get our gear, grab breakfast, and get to the bus stop at the tour desk. It may be close, so let's hurry."

"Okay, our sleeping bags are in the SUV. I will meet

you there in about five minutes with our backpacks. Meanwhile, have you changed the batteries in our headlamps?"

"I'll do it when I check the sleeping bags and arrange our camera gear. I'll put a fresh battery in the camera too. Yesterday's is in the charger."

"Right."

They moved rapidly. At the food court, after wolfing down breakfasts with plenty of protein, they filled their mugs with hot chocolate and walked quickly across the front courtyard to the bus. They had only five minutes to spare.

+ + +

Both Andy and Abby had previously done cross-country skiing at Big Bear Lake in the San Bernardino Mountains. As they rode the bus up the grade towards Badger Pass, they decided they would probably bring the kids the next time they went trekking.

After checking in at the Badger Pass Ski Center and the National Park Service A-Frame building, Andy and Abby set out down the Glacier Point road. The road was not plowed beyond Badger Pass during the winter, but it was groomed regularly. At the A-frame, they learned that the road had been groomed only a few days earlier and was in good shape.

Most of the time, they used an automatic focus wide-angle lens to take pictures of one another and the scenery. When they got to the Sentinel Dome trail head, however, they spotted several animals. Abby handed Andy the telephoto zoom lens from the leather case on her belt. "Just a reminder – since we're using auto-ISO, why don't you shoot manually at a high shutter speed and smaller aperture?"

He nodded. "I was thinking the same thing, but this

camera does it automatically, depending upon the focal length. Isn't that a fox over there?" He pointed. Abby turned to look as he made an image. A marmot emerged, scurrying across the snow as the fox chased it. Their camera clicked rapidly as images of the chase were captured.

Since it was still early afternoon, they went up to Taft Point. Leading the way, Andy moved slowly. "This close to the cliffs, let's be extra careful. This granite feels icy."

Abby grunted. "Let's take off our skis and stay well away from the edge. Even from here, we've got great views of both El Capitan and Yosemite Falls. Let me have the camera."

Andy stopped and gave it to her. "That wide angle will be okay with both of them, but let's get out the macro and shoot both El Cap and the falls with it as well." He reached around and got it out of his backpack.

"That's a good idea. Then I'll leave it on the camera. We passed some snow plants back there a ways."

They skied and took pictures at a leisurely pace, and then they went on to Sentinel Dome. At the base of the dome, they took off their skis before hiking up to the top. While there, they took some pictures while munching on energy bars. It was mid-afternoon when they headed down to Glacier Point.

That night, the ski hut was full to capacity. Everyone was talking about the bright light in the previous night's sky. A man in his twenties said, "I read in the San Francisco Chronicle that because of the ban on nuclear weapons testing, it should not have been some kind of test."

An older African-American woman nodded. "There

were many speculations about what could have been the source of the light. There's been no response from the Pentagon up to this point."

A man with a gray beard nodded. "I doubt that our government will admit anything if we're involved. We may not get any answers for months – if at all."

There were murmurs of agreement all around the shelter. Andy and Abby simply listened silently.

9.
Solving a Problem

The van's flight away from the Earth to beyond the atmosphere before exploding was frequently discussed privately. They agreed at the beginning to discuss it only in person and not via email or telephone. It turned into a major faith challenge and struggle for all four of them. Days stretched into weeks.

Richard and Char got no answers when casting lots about the van, and that surprised and disappointed them. They found their friendships with Andy and Abby were growing stronger. No one was sure what they should do, if anything, in the aftermath. The flash in the sky continued to draw speculation in the media almost every day because it had been seen throughout most of the western hemisphere.

One evening after Bible study, the four of them were sitting in Richard and Char's living room, quietly discussing what had become both their favorite and the least favorite subject. Char raised her index finger. "I have an idea. ... Richard and I have the privilege of friendship with former President Everett Williams and his wife Jane. They are both devout Christians. Why don't we cast lots to see if we should take them into our confidence?"

Richard smiled. "Excellent!"

Char excused herself for a moment, and she returned carrying a small pouch containing the three old quarters they used for casting lots. Richard went to a little rocker switch near the front door, and when he pressed it, hidden motors closed the drapes on all the downstairs windows.

The four of them got on their knees. Char began, saying, "Father. We're glad that Richard and I were witnesses to this miracle, and we're pleased that you enabled us to have a small role in that drama. We've been wrestling with our faith ever since, Lord."

Richard continued. "We're trying to comprehend your will and purpose in all of this. Tonight, will you please help us understand through the casting of lots?"

Heads-Heads-Heads.

Richard picked up the coins. "Lord, do you want this miracle to be part of the testimonies of all four of us?"

Heads-Heads-Heads.

Char picked up the coins. "Jesus, do you want Richard and I to introduce Abby and Andy to former President Everett Williams and his wife, Jane?"

Heads-Heads-Heads.

Richard picked up the coins. "Master, will you use the former President and his wife to prophesy to the four of us?"

Heads-Heads-Heads.

Char picked up the coins. "Heavenly Father, the first time Richard and I cast lots, I was skeptical, and because of that I arrogantly asked you for a sign to show us that we were on the right path. I know you forgave me for that, and you answered my prayers. This is the first time that Abby and Andy have been with us when we have cast lots, and though they trust you, Lord, they're understandably skeptical. Will you please do something tonight to affirm your love for them?"

Heads-Heads-Heads.

Richard spoke softly. Thank you, thank you, Lord.

You have blessed us countless times and in untold ways, and all we can do at this point is thank you and praise you. Speaking on behalf of the others and myself, we thank you and praise you in Jesus' name. Amen."

None of them spoke at first. Then Andy said, "Awesome! We need to go outside. Yes! We need to!" He stood up, reached down and took Abby's hand, and helped her up. The four of them walked to the front door, opened it, and walked out on the sidewalk to the curbing at the street. Char smiled. "It's cool out here, but it's a beautiful night."

Abby nodded. "Yes. Look!" She pointed.

Without warning, the sky was filled with the Aurora Borealis (northern lights). Simultaneously, the lights went out all over Southern California. Several minutes later, the lights came back on, and the Northern Lights disappeared.

"Awesome!" Andy was grinning. "Praise God, from whom all blessings flow!"

Abby nodded. "Amen!"

Richard and Char nodded as well. "Amen!"

They went back inside. Richard beaconed. "Let's go to the theater and see what the media response is."

It took a few minutes for the projector to warm up. Char quickly found a news bulletin was being broadcast. "... We go now to Mervin Eddison, who recently retired as the chief astronomer at the Palomar Observatory and is currently a consultant for this station. Dr. Eddison, what can you tell us about this unexpected display of the Northern Lights?"

The astronomer was talking on a cell phone but hung up. He shook his gray head vigorously. "There can be no immediate explanation for this. I just made a phone call to a friend of mine, and he is as baffled as I am. He did tell me something else that was also unexpected."

"What's that, Dr. Eddison?"

"When it happened, he was working with a communications technician. As you know, we've been having difficulties with our communications satellites ever since that mysterious flash of light several weeks ago. My friend told me that after the Aurora Borealis appeared and disappeared this evening, our communications satellites suddenly seemed no longer to have those difficulties. I can perhaps supply more information tomorrow after I talk to some of my colleagues."

"Thank you, Dr. Eddison. We now go to Carl Sampson, who is a power engineer with Southern California Edison, with a report on the lights here in Southern California. Mr. Sampson?"

"Good evening, Sarah. During the prolonged winter several years ago we used to power down the streetlights throughout the country to conserve power at night. Those power shifts did not affect the power within commercial buildings, hospitals, homes, or apartments. Evidently, the same thing happened tonight throughout at least this part of the state, but it was unplanned, and I've been unable to find anyone responsible. It is another mystery. I put in a call to Pacific Gas and Electric, but I've not heard back from them yet."

"Thank you, Mr. Sampson. Please keep investigating, and let us know what you find out."

"I will."

Richard muted the sound. "All that God does, God does well. God answered our prayer."

"Amen!"

+ + +

The following Thursday, late in the morning, Andy's phone buzzed in his office. "Yes, Janet?"

"Char Donovan is on line two."

He picked up his phone. "Good morning, Char. How are you?"

"Good morning Andy, I'm blessed. I am calling because Abby is with the kids and cannot come to the phone now, and Richard is practicing downstairs. I've talked to former First Lady Janet Williams earlier this morning, and the four of us are to be their guests this weekend at their ranch."

"Do you mean their ranch near Gorman, about thirty miles north of the Magic Mountain amusement park?"

"Yes. They live there most of the time since he retired from politics. Abby's Mom and Dad will be at your house in time for lunch tomorrow, and your Mom will join them. They are going to take care of all of our kids while we're off for the weekend. Richard and I will pick up you and Abby at 2:00 so that we'll have plenty of time to relax at the ranch before dinner."

Andy leaned back in his chair. "This sounds great. I'm really looking forward to meeting them. I've admired them for as long as I can remember."

"The former First Lady said that she was looking forward to meeting you two as well. No one knew it, but the two of them put on disguises and went to the concert we did to benefit the hospital."

"Really? I never dreamed they would be there!"

"If you want, they have 4K video of that concert and a few other concerts that we can enjoy."

Andy smiled. "Char, you and Richard are a real blessing to Abby and me."

"You two are a blessing to us as well. By the way,

Andy, anytime Richard and I are away from home, there's a security detail that watches over our children. While we're gone for the weekend, that detail will be watching all the children at your folks' house."

Andy scowled. "You'll have to explain that to us when we see you."

Char laughed. "No worries, Andy. Richard and I have had to put up with it for so long, we kind of take it for granted. It saved our bacon a time or two."

"Really!" Andy's secretary, Janet, came to his door and waved at him. "Char, my secretary is waving at me, so I'll have to get off of the phone. I'll see you tomorrow about 2:00, okay?"

"Right. See you then."

"The Board Meeting starts in about five minutes." Janet raised her eyebrows. "You'll need to get moving if you're going to be on time."

"Thanks!" Andy nodded. Grabbing a folder, he headed out the door.

+ + +

The large SUV that transported them up to Gorman was almost as comfortable as a limousine. Their driver was an Air Force lieutenant, as was another man, who rode up front on the right. After introducing the two men to Andy and Abby, they got in, and Char explained.

"When we met President Williams at the White House when we got back from our honeymoon, he told General Oswald that, from then on, Richard and I were to have a security detail. At the time, General Oswald was Chairman of the Join Chiefs, so that was no problem for him. Even after President Williams left office, however, the security detail has continued. It's not quite as involved as it once was because we're not in the news as much as we were right after we were

114

married."

Andy nodded. "You said on the phone yesterday that they had saved your bacon a time or two. Can you elaborate?"

Richard nodded. "We can now, because a few years have passed. One time we were at the Long Beach mall with our neighbors and all our kids, and a man approached Char selling so-called 'insurance' or 'security.'"

Char nodded. "I politely told him that our security was enough, but he was rather insistent. One of our friends approached, wanting to know if everything was all right, and the man backed off. My cell phone rang, and I was asked if there was a problem. I simply told the officer who was currently in command of our security detail what happened and what the man had said."

Richard smiled. "That evening a black SUV pulled up and several rather large men got out. One of the Marines in our detail came out of our yard's foliage and asked if there was something he could help them with. One of those big men reached inside of his coat, and within seconds, those six men from the SUV were on the ground and bleeding. They didn't get off a shot."

Andy stared. "Then what?"

"I went out on our porch, and the Captain of our detail simply said that they had taken care of our problem and would clean things up quickly. They did."

"Wow!" Abby smiled.

During the remainder of the drive up to Gorman, they talked about a lot of things. Richard told about a couple of concerts he had done the previous weekend. "Long Beach City College has a nice little auditorium with excellent acoustics and seats a little over a thousand. They have a very nice Steinway. On Friday night I did a benefit concert there, sponsored by an anonymous donor. It was all classical, and it was sold out. I enjoyed that audience, and the reception afterward was very nice."

Andy smiled. "How much were the tickets?"

"I think they ran from $100 to $500 dollars." He paused. "Saturday night I performed at another community college – El Camino. The auditorium is a little larger, and my performance was part of an annual concert series. Arthur Rubenstein once played on the same piano I played on. Many in the audience were music students from local high schools and colleges. It was fun for Char and me to chat with them afterward"

Char nodded. "It was enjoyable, but exhausting. Those kids had endless questions!"

Andy smiled. "There's one thing I can tell you that I think you two will find interesting. Abby got a kick out of hearing about it."

Richard cocked his head. "What happened?"

"After the aurora borealis incident, calls for pain medication at our hospital from the nurses decreased significantly – almost half."

"Really!"

He nodded. "I had Janice, my secretary put in a few calls to the administrators of some other hospitals here in Southern California. They all had similar experiences."

It was late afternoon as they drove off of Interstate 5, up into the hills above Gorman, and onto the Williams ranch. As they passed one fence, Abby noticed some soldiers under the trees nearby, but they saw no other obvious signs of security. Their driver pointed. "That's probably the only outward sign of security you'll see today unless we have an emergency and go into lock down mode. In that situation, there would be very few places in this country - other than the White House, of course - that are safer than here."

Abby gazed out the window. "It's over 4000 feet here, so they get snow in the winter. There was quite a blanket of it here a few months ago. Now it's wildflowers. I love it!"

A few moments later, they arrived at a large, sprawling ranch house. Everett and Janet Williams came out to greet their guests. After the warm greetings of old friends and new, Richard pointed. "I had forgotten, Mr. President, how colorful the wildflowers can be up here at this time of the year."

Everett Williams smiled. "Yes, this year the flowers seem especially colorful. I think that last summer's brush fires may have something to do with it."

Abby pointed. "Those are California Poppies, aren't they?"

The former first lady smiled. "Yes, the gold-colored flowers are poppies. There are also some creamcups and tidylips."

Char pointed in another direction. "Over there are a lot of chocolate lilies and sky lupines. I love lupines!"

The former first lady put her arm around Char and took Abby's hand. "Come on, dinner will be ready soon. I'll give you a quick tour, and then we'll give you a chance to freshen up before we eat." As she proceeded to give her guests a rapid tour of the enormous ranch house, the men followed along.

Less than a half-hour later, they heard the clang of a bell. President Williams held up his hand. "That's a salvaged bell that I got from the wreck of an old three-masted sailing ship. It's kind of a ten-minute warning. Your suitcases are in the guest rooms we showed you.

You can join us on the patio when you're ready." They all went their separate ways.

For dinner, they gathered around a large round table about ten yards from a swimming pool and hot-tub area. At Janet's request, Richard offered a blessing, and they began attacking their salads. Andy looked across the table at the former President and First Lady. "The four of us have been having a faith struggle with something that happened recently, and it was Char's suggestion that we sit down and talk with the two of you about it."

Char swallowed and nodded. "We have talked with one another about it privately, and we've not taken the risk of using telephones or email."

The former president nodded. "Our staff here at the ranch has high security clearance, but considering my experiences with you and Richard, I think we should wait until after dinner to discuss whatever is bothering you. Then we'll talk about it in my study behind closed doors."

Andy nodded. "Good. We appreciate that."

For more than an hour, they talked about a variety of things as they ate. The former president asked Richard and Char about the history behind casting lots to determine divine will. Janet Williams was curious about an article in the *Los Angeles Times* she had read concerning the incident at the zoo.

After dessert, they went to the President's study. It was a large windowless room, with books and presidential memorabilia lining the walls. They sat down in a comfortable conversation pit made up of overstuffed chairs and love seats.

The former president leaned back in his custom-made chair and smiled. "Now we have privacy. Who wants to begin?"

Andy held Abby's hand as he began. "This past winter Abby and I took a much-anticipated and much-needed vacation in Yosemite Valley, and we stayed at the lodge. One evening we decided to have dinner at Yosemite View Lodge just outside the park, and the dinner was truly memorable. By the time we were finished, the rain had stopped, and the sky was clearing as we returned to the valley. We did some landscape astrophotography, making starlight images in several places."

Andy paused, and Abby continued. "As we finished making some images of Yosemite Falls under a canopy of stars, we drove east, and as we approached the Yosemite Chapel area, a car sped out of the parking lot in an obvious hurry. We thought it was strange, and as we got next to the chapel's parking area, we could see a van parked at the rear of the area."

Janet Williams nodded. "Were there other cars in the lot or any sign of other people?"

Andy shook his head. "It was getting close to midnight, so everything was quiet. The only light was from the porch light of the chapel because it was a new moon that night."

"Go on." The former President was totally focused. "Were Richard and Char with you?"

Abby shook her head. "No."

Andy continued. "I felt uneasy, as though something was wrong, and I told Abby that as we got out of our SUV. As we approached the van, there was no sign of life. As I looked in one of the windows, I could see a dull red glow on the ceiling of the van. When I opened the side door, we saw a large rectangular shape in the middle of the floor. The two of us got in and peered over the top of the container. I saw a countdown timer with less than thirty minutes. With my flashlight, I examined everything I could see in the container, and my heart was in my throat." Andy stopped.

Abby leaned against him and looked at his face. "We've got to tell them everything, Andy, just as it happened."

Andy nodded. "Mr. President, I was trained at Eglin Air Force Base on the basics of bomb construction and deactivation. I had seen pictures of something like this, but this was a real, operational, thermonuclear device."

The eyes of the former president and first lady got huge as Andy continued. "Abby and I realized that there was no time for evacuation, and there was no time to get a bomb crew there. In that pressure cooker environment we decided to call Char and Richard, and, praise God, we got a good cell phone connection." Abby nodded and squeezed his hand.

Richard took over. "We put our phones on the speaker-phone, and Andy asked us to cast lots for them to see what they should do."

The former first lady was startled. "Really!"

Richard nodded. "Char asked, 'Lord, will you help us in this emergency?' and we got heads-heads-heads. I asked if Andy should try to disarm the bomb, and it was tails-tails-tails. Char asked if Abby should try to disarm the bomb, and it was tails-tails-tails. I asked if we should just pray, and it was tails-tails-tails."

Char nodded. "Richard and I were stunned and couldn't speak for a moment. Andy asked us if we were still there, and Richard said yes while I prayed silently. Suddenly, just as surely as we are sitting here I knew what I had to ask. I asked, 'Master should Andy simply command the bomb and van to be gone?' I picked up

120

the coins and cast them, and it was heads-heads-heads."

Abby grinned. "I was absolutely stunned. I said, 'You have GOT to be kidding!'"

Andy nodded. "We put our cell phone on a small boulder near us. I put my hands on the van. I will never forget the prayer I prayed, because it didn't seem to come from me. I heard myself say this: 'Heavenly Father, we're standing on your promises and, more specifically on the promise of your Son, Jesus, Our Savior. ... In the precious and powerful name of Jesus, your Son, and Our Savior, we command this van to be gone, leaving this Earth and its atmosphere. Alleluia! Amen!' Abby and I fell backward as the van sailed upward, and it was almost immediately out of sight."

Abby nodded. "We talked to Char and Richard a bit longer. We went into the chapel and prayed, and then we went back to our van in the parking lot."

Andy nodded. "Mr. President, as Abby was getting into the van, you can guess what happened."

Startled, he asked. "I can?" He paused. "Oh" His eyes grew big. "My God!" He paused. "The flash!" They all looked at each other in silence. "This puts a spin on that incident that I could never have imagined!"

10.
A Secret Solution

"The last time I felt this way, Janet and I were living in the White House, and we learned that Yellowstone was about to become a volcano." The former president paused. "Richard, you and Char got no answers from casting lots at first, yet Our Lord has led the four of you here. I have no doubt of that."

Char nodded. "We thought of telling General Oswald, but we decided not to do so until we talked with you."

He nodded. He got up, and he went to the love seat where Janet was seated. He sat down again and closed his eyes. Janet put her hand on his and also closed her eyes. They sat there praying silently for several minutes.

Janet opened her eyes. "Char, do you and Richard have any engagements next weekend?" The former president opened his eyes and nodded.

Richard shook his head. "We're rehearsing and getting ready for some engagements next month. Why do you ask?"

The former president looked at his new friends. "Abby, Andy, I want to keep the two of you out of this as much as possible. It may not work out that way, but I'll do my best. General Oswald was at Beale Air Force Base north of Sacramento when the flash occurred, and he stayed there until the day before yesterday. Now he's at Edwards Air Force Base, not far from here." He paused briefly. "Wait! I have a better idea! Janet, it's a nice warm evening out there. Why don't the five of you go out and have some fun? I have some calls to make. I'll fill all of you in when I've made my calls."

They all stood up. As Everett Williams went to his desk and his phone, the other five went out. Janet was mildly amused. "When I see my husband get a gleam in his eye like that, I know he's come up with something good."

In his study, the former president picked up his phone's handset, punched a number, sat down, and leaned back in his chair. "Good evening, General. This is Everett."

"Good afternoon, Mr. President, what can I do for you?"

"I think I've found a way to get to the truth regarding that flash in the sky a few weeks ago, but we'll need help in coordinating agency efforts to deal with the media and the public."

"Are you serious?"

"Yes. You know that I have contacts all over the world, and some information has come to me in an unexpected and new way."

"What information?"

"I know this is a secure line, but let's not get ahead of ourselves my friend."

"What do you suggest?"

"I think speculation on this has gone on far too long, and I want us to move fast, though I have no legal right to make it happen. I'd like to get representatives from the White House, Homeland Security, and the CIA together, in person if possible."

"Is this information that good?"

"My word of honor, General, yes."

The General paused, stunned. "Oh. That's

different." The general paused again. "I'll call you back in a few minutes." The connection ended.

Everett Williams leaned further back in his chair, put his feet up on the desk, and picked up a novel called *The Gaardian Saga* [©2015], which he had been reading for several days. He finished reading a chapter and most of another chapter before the phone rang.

"Hello. General?"

"Yes, Mr. President. I've been considering how you said you wanted to move quickly, and how among your guests at the ranch are the Donovans. Without disclosing anything on the phone, Mr. President, may I safely assume that they are somehow either directly or indirectly involved in this?"

General Oswald could not see the former president smile. "I won't deny that, my friend." He took his feet down from his desk.

There was a pause. "Mr. President, with one of my calls, I issued an order, and your ranch is now locked down. You will have five more guests tomorrow morning. I will be among them. Will that be a problem?"

"Of course not! I will see you then."

"Absolutely." The connection ended.

He slapped his desk. "Yes! Thank you Lord!" He rose from his desk and headed for the pool area to join the others.

Richard looked up to see the former president approaching and waved. "Success?"

He smiled. "Yes. The ranch is now locked down because of additional guests who will be arriving during the early morning hours. Meanwhile, I need to have you and Char get together and discuss how you can tell the story, strictly from your perspective, without mentioning your friends' names."

Abby approached. "What's happening?"

President Williams looked at her. "The ranch is now locked down, and when some additional guests arrive, it's important that you and Andy stay out of sight there in the south wing. I'll have Janet stay with you and keep you amused. She's extremely good at this kind of thing."

Dripping from the pool and wiping himself off, Andy approached. "Did I hear you say that Janet is going to keep us amused for a while?"

The president nodded. "When Char arranged for this visit, the names of you and your husband were not listed. Since we were not in lock-down when you came in, we did not make even a visual record of your presence. You won't leave until after we're out of lock-down." As Char approached, he turned back to Richard. "I want you and Char to tell the story of a phone call you received, but you won't identify the callers. General Oswald knows they are friends, but that's all."

Andy smiled. "I like this! I hope it works!"

"It will be a load off of my mind." Abby nodded.

+ + +

Just after 10:00 the next morning, Char smiled when she and Richard finished telling the story. "When the call ended, he and I prayed and cast lots. When the light outside our bedroom window lit up, Richard and I opened our eyes and nodded at each other. We knew what caused that bright light in the sky."

Richard nodded. "We knew it was the van we had been told about. We prayed a while longer, and then we turned off the light and went to sleep."

There was silence as everyone in President Williams' office looked at one another. He spoke quietly. "Now you know why I asked General Oswald to gather all of you here at the ranch."

The general spoke authoritatively. "I've discussed this with both Admiral Patton and Admiral Schultz. We all agree that since the man and woman wish to remain anonymous, we see no need to have their names on record."

Several of them disagreed. The head of Homeland Security, Sam Jessup, was adamant. "How do we know we can trust these two people? We need to check their backgrounds thoroughly for potential security risks."

"Nonsense!" The general was firm. "I've been dealing with the Donovans for years, and this man and woman are among thousands that my staff has cleared over the last decade simply because anyone associated with the Donovans has to have a security check."

President Williams nodded. "Just after Mount Yellowstone began to erupt, I ordered General Grommond to develop security parameters for Richard and Char. The Donovans are a security asset."

Richard grinned. "Char and I are glad, too. We've had a few incidents where security was there when we needed it, but we have our privacy as well. General, about how many secured people do Char and I have on your list of secured friends for us?"

He cleared his throat. "In the U.S., there're more than two thousand. When we add your contacts on five other continents, we've cleared more than double that."

Several of them stared at him. Sam Jessup was incredulous. "Five other continents - are you serious?"

Char burst out laughing. "Of course, he's serious! The only continent where Richard and I have not performed is Antarctica!" There were smiles all around the room.

Everett Williams lifted a hand. "There will be speculation for years as to the source and reason for the flash in the sky, no matter what. It seems to me, we have at least two choices. First, we can shut down the various investigations going on in the government and not offer the public an explanation. The other is to shut down the investigations and tell the public a simple lie."

General Oswald looked at his friend. "What kind of lie do you have in mind, Mr. President?"

"A satellite with a nuclear-power supply began to fall out of orbit, so it was ordered to self-destruct."

A tall woman with flaming red hair shook her head. "I wouldn't be able to sell our President on that. Telling the public that we have nuclear-powered satellites above us will panic many people, including some of our allies."

Some of them nodded, including the general. "I agree. It will be relatively simple to shut down the investigations going on, telling each agency that another agency figured out what happened. The public will continue to speculate. Can all of us in this room agree that what we've discussed will remain in this room, and that there will be no record?"

After discussing it for almost an hour, Richard and Char were relieved that the reason for the meeting and all that was said would be officially forgotten.

Thirty minutes later, a Boeing CH-47 Chinook helicopter landed on a helipad next to the ranch house. Hovering above was a Boeing AH-64 attack helicopter. General Oswald escorted the special visitors back to Edwards Air Force Base.

President Williams, along with Char and Richard, walked from the helipad over to the pool. The others were coming out of the south wing of the house with refreshments in their hands. They were all smiling, and the former president gave Janet a kiss. "Everything is settled. Officially, that meeting did not take place."

Andy's mouth dropped open. "Really?"

He nodded. "You and Abby are deep in the shadows of recent history, unidentified except for present company. All the investigating agencies will be told that all questions had been answered, with the results analyzed, but it will all remain secret, with details in the hands of another agency, which won't be identified."

Char nodded. "You and Abby are among thousands that are on a list of our friends who have been cleared for security, and at the meeting, Richard and I simply told the story of a phone call we had received from a couple of our friends, who we did not identify."

Abby shook her head. "If someone really wanted to identify us, couldn't they?"

Richard shook his head. "Just before General Oswald took off just now, I asked him if there was any kind of record of something flying into the sky that night. He said that a UFO was initially identified that night from an elevation of three thousand meters and moving away from the Earth, but where it came from could not be identified. No one else knows either the identity of that UFO or where it came from."

Janet stood up. "Let's go inside. The lock down will probably not be lifted for at least another hour or two. Everett and I have a 4K video of that benefit concert with The Magnificent Seven and the Donovans. Everett and I haven't seen it yet because we were there for the live performance. Our home theater is this way - come on!" They all went inside.

+ + +

Monday morning, before the Donovans and the Hickmans started down the mountain, everyone feasted on a large breakfast buffet. The fruits, pancakes, meats, and potatoes were delicious, but Abby and Andy were both surprised and delighted with eggs *au buerre noir*. Abby had seconds. "I've never had eggs like this, Janet. How are they fixed?"

"Everett and I first experience this Creole dish when we were in the White House. The sauce over the eggs is made of browned butter and vinegar. I think our cook adds capers to the seasoning."

Char nodded. "I've fixed them a few times for Richard and me when we've had a relaxing morning. Eggs with all that butter are so rich we don't do it very often."

While the Hickmans and Donovans finished their breakfasts and relaxed, their SUV was loaded with the luggage. Then Everett and Janet Williams gave all four of them hugs with their good-byes before the four clamored into the SUV. Since the ranch was no longer in lock-down, there was once again very little evidence of the high security that surrounded them.

As the SUV pulled off the access in Gorman and onto the Interstate 5 freeway, Richard looked at Char. "This has been a wonderful break, but we'll be joining the seven again in less than two weeks."

Char nodded. "I checked our email this morning, and Tom Dobbins sent us a message with some new arrangements attached."

"Really! Excellent!"

Andy cocked his head. "What do you mean, 'new arrangements'?"

Char smiled. "Both times we have performed together, we've had a few songs that are arranged just for us. They're songs that are currently among the most popular or recently popular. We also drop off some songs that are older and no longer as popular."

Richard nodded. "Some of the time, friends of ours, or friends of the seven send us arrangements to consider through Bobbi Zealand, our manager. In this case, though, the arrangements are from Tom Dobbins."

Char smiled again. "After we did that reunion concert in Long Beach, we all decided that we wanted to get together as a group about once a year or so. Bobbi Zealand has suggested that since each of us has our own careers and album sales, these reunion concerts will always be benefits for recognized charities. Next will be a concert for Samaritan's Purse disaster relief. I think the following year we're doing a benefit for a combination of agencies that supply food for world hunger relief."

Richard nodded. "I was out of the country when Cedar Fair Entertainment proposed that we do a concert a Hollywood Bowl. Char, Abby, and the kids were visiting at Knott's Berry Farm when they offered the proposal. We refused because it was not to be a benefit."

Abby looked out the window and pointed. "Not far from here, near Westwood Village, is UCLA and their Medical Center. Andy's going to be giving a lecture next month, aren't you, Andy?"

He nodded. "Yes, but it won't really be a lecture. It will be a presentation, and it is going to be somewhat unusual. It has been very difficult finding funding for a double-blind study on the effectiveness of prayer."

Surprised, Char raised her eyebrows. "There's going to be a study on the effectiveness of prayer?"

Andy nodded. "We're going to try to duplicate a study done a long time ago in Texas. I'm making this presentation because I did the research for the grant proposal. We're going to study three groups of orthopedic patients who have similar surgeries. The chaplains will follow three carefully planned scripts, one for each person in each of the three groups."

Richard nodded. "I assume people in one of the three groups will be approached with the standard visits by the chaplains for all patients."

Andy nodded. "That is correct. In the second group, the patients will also be told that there will be church folks praying for them while they are in the hospital."

Char smiled. "And the third group of patients will be told more?"

He nodded. "Patients in the third group will be told that, if they give permission, there will be people praying for them as individuals. The people praying will be given a special patient number, instead of a name. With that number will be details about the kind of surgery, and about the day and time it is taking place. Those people praying will also be given updates, describing the recovery process."

Richard was fascinated. "What will be studied and analyzed?"

"There will be ways of measuring the recovery progress in terms of percentage and time. The total number of calls for nurse assistance will be recorded, along with patient descriptions of their level of pain from one to ten. Their number of requests for pain medication will also be counted. The UCLA students assisting with the study will record the data by the patient number, and a different group of students will compile the data, and then all the data will be analyzed by a third team. The study done years ago, that I mentioned, followed the same procedures, only it was before hospitals were all digitalized for record keeping."

"Wow! That sounds really involved," Char blurted. "How soon will you know the results?"

Andy smiled. "It will at least take several months, maybe much longer."

11.
An Emergency and Anonymity

After church the following Sunday, Andy and Abby took his mother to lunch at the Long Beach Mall. The kids loved talking with Grandma while they ate. Afterward, Trina invited her grand kids to come and play in her yard for a while.

While Toby and Joey played on the lawn, the adults sat under a large avocado tree. Grandma Trina was in her element. "I got a call last Wednesday from Malcolm Everly, a reporter from the Press–Telegram. He wants to write a feature article on Huck and I, for the anniversary of his going home to heaven."

Abby spoke quietly. "I didn't realize that it has been five years, Mom. How are you feeling?"

She smiled. "I'm fine, actually! I have such precious memories of Huck. I think I'll enjoy sharing them again. When Huck and I first married, our age difference was a huge chat and gossip subject. We both had to make new friends, because so many of our friends before our marriage felt uncomfortable with us. We had thirty-five wonderful years of blessings that I will get to share now with current readers of the paper. Malcolm is going to come here tomorrow morning and interview me. Later, he'll talk to pastor Paul and some of the other pastors in town who knew Huck. When he asked about our children, I told him that his oldest was a hospital administrator, and he'll want to talk to you, Andy."

He nodded. "Okay. That should not be a problem."

She shook her head. "Andy, that's not my point. I want you with me when he interviews me tomorrow morning."

He was silent and stared straight ahead. Abby put her hand on his, and they both closed their eyes for over a minute. Abby smiled. "The Lord will guide you, Mom, and you're right, Andy should probably be here with you."

Later, it was time to leave, and they held hands while the kids stumbled ahead towards the car. Andy put his arms around his Mom. "See you tomorrow morning. I'll be here about 8:30. I'll plan to not be in the office before noon."

"Okay." She turned to Abby after she finished strapping the kids into their car seats. "I always love it when you come over, Abby. You're really good for my son and for me as well."

"I love you too, Mom. Your love comes through Andy."

As they drove away, Abby asked, "Are you going to tell the journalist about Huck's gift that he's passed on to you?"

"I don't know, but probably not. Down through the generations, we've not told many people about it." His cell phone rang. "Would you answer that for me?"

"Sure." She took his phone out of his jacket pocket. "Hello?"

"Andy Hickman, please."

"He's driving. I'm his wife. Can I help you?"

"Yes. Please come to the hospital immediately. This is Joe Bahnmiller of the United States Secret Service. Come directly to the Emergency Ward. You're both cleared to get past our security detail. A police officer will be there to take them to Char Carpenter. She and

134

her husband Richard are already here. Please come quickly."

"Okay." The connection ended. "That was someone from The Secret Service, Andy. Go to the hospital's Emergency Ward. Richard and Char are already there. "

"Did you say, The Secret Service? What are they doing there? Could it be Janet or Everett Williams?"

"I don't know."

When they arrived at the emergency entrance, Char was standing there with two men. She went to the driver's side door. "Hi Andy. I'll park the car and take care of the kids. You and Abby go on inside."

As Andy and Abby moved towards the doors, there were flashes, video camera lights, and media workers crowding around. As questions were shouted at them, they both kept responding, "No comment!"

Inside, in the waiting room, it was quieter, but not by very much. A man approached them. "I'm Joe Bahnmiller. You must be the Hickmans."

Andy nodded. "What's going on?"

"Please just come with me." As he moved towards the interior access door, it opened, and they went in. Considering the previous times they had been there, the ward seemed completely normal. Andy and Abby were led to the last room at the end of a hallway, and the curtain was pulled back.

Beside a gurney with a vaguely familiar-looking patient, Richard Donovan stood there with a woman who also looked somewhat familiar. Abby froze and clutched Andy's arm. "Dear Lord! Aren't you the First Lady, Janelle Riley?"

There was no color to her face, and she looked like she hadn't slept in weeks, with her eyes red and swollen. The First Lady nodded and spoke quietly. "Yes,

I'm Janelle Riley. When I first got here I asked for the Donovans, and I'm glad they came." She looked up at Richard.

"When Char and I saw the situation, we immediately knew that you and Andy were needed."

Andy nodded. "Richard is this perhaps part of what you and Char prophesied?"

Richard looked at him squarely. "We think so."

Andy stepped forward and took the First Lady's hand. "It is good to meet you, but I'm sorry it is under these circumstances." Abby stepped up, and he introduced her. "This is my wife, Abby. Abby, the First Lady." They shook hands. "Ma'am, We do not know what the situation is. No one has told us anything."

The First Lady nodded. "My husband and I had just arrived at a large home, not far from here, on Ocean Avenue. He turned to wave at the crowd, and a shot rang out as a bullet went into the center of his chest."

Andy's eyes grew wide. "Lord!"

"We were brought here in a matter of less than five minutes. This is a marvelous hospital! While they worked on him, I called Richard Donovan because I knew that he and his wife live near here." She stopped to swallow. "My husband was stable until about ten minutes ago, and they brought him back here because ICU was already full. Then his heart stopped."

Richard put his hand on her shoulder. "The media know nothing yet. She told Dr. Cochran to hold everything until you got there. Since you're the administrator, he has complied, but we can't hold things off much longer. It's up to you, Andy."

He reached for Abby's hand, and they closed their eyes. Then without speaking, he and Abby opened their eyes and turned to the gurney. Andy put his other hand on top of the President's chest, and Abby put her other hand on top of his. They closed their eyes again. "Heavenly Father, contrary to what Richard said, it's not up to me. It's up to you. Abby and I are here according to your will. May your will be done."

They were completely still for several minutes. They were aware of warmth permeating them and flowing through them onto the President. Suddenly, the President began coughing violently and sat up.

The First Lady shouted, "Doctor! Nurse! Come here! Quickly!"

The President continued to cough as John Cochran raced in with two nurses behind him. Andy and Abby stepped back as the Doctor grabbed the President's shoulders. As he did, President Riley stopped coughing. "Aren't you the doctor who worked on me when I first got here?" He nodded. "I vaguely remember.... I turned to wave at the crowd, and then there was incredible pain in my chest. I came in here. I saw you. The next thing I know I'm coughing my head off."

"Mr. President, I need to examine you again. Andy, you, Abby, and your friend, please give me room to work." He turned to the first lady. "You can stay if you wish, but I need room for myself and my nurses. Why don't you go ahead and sit down? This will take a few minutes." She did so as the others left.

In the hall, Andy spoke. "Abby, Richard, come with me back to my office." They walked out of the Emergency Room's rear hallway exit. "Richard, get Char on the phone and see how soon she can meet us at the east entrance."

"Right." He took out his phone and dialed. "Hi. We need to leave. Where are you?"

"I've been driving around, trying to avoid the

media."

"Good. Meet us at the east entrance okay?"

"I'll be there in a couple of minutes."

"Good." He put away his phone. "She'll meet us there in a couple of minutes."

Outside Andy's office, they stopped, and he said, "Wait here." Going in, he greeted his secretary. "Hi Janet."

"Hi!"

"There's no time to explain now. I'm not in, you don't know where I've gone, and you don't know when I'll be back. Things may get hectic for you, but I know you can handle it."

She nodded. "Is the President dead?"

"No, praise God! I'll see you when I see you."

"Right."

He turned and quickly left. The three of them went out the door just as Char drove up. They quickly squeezed in with the kids. Andy spoke hurriedly. "Go to your car. We'll follow you to your place, okay?"

Char nodded and sped ahead.

"That's a good idea, Andy. Char, go straight for a couple of blocks and then go around." Richard took out his phone. "Security, this is Richard. Code four. We'll be home in less than ten with Andy and Abby Hickman. They'll need full provisions."

"Code four is confirmed. You'll have a full escort to the top of the hill. Another crew will handle provisions."

"Thanks." He put away his phone, just as they pulled up next to their car. "You can follow us up Cherry, and try to stay fairly close. Our garage will take your car as well as our SUV. Pull right on in."

Abby put her hand on Char's arm. "Thank you."

Char grinned. "Don't thank us yet. We may have lots

of fun ahead before we're in the house and secure, but don't worry. Do you see that jeep there at the corner?"

Andy nodded. "Sure."

"They will pull in behind you, and you may see some other vehicles join our little train. It's all normal." Char got out, and Andy moved into the driver's seat. Abby got in beside him.

Richard started rolling as soon as Char had closed her door. They went north until they got to Seventh Street and turned right. As Andy turned, a van coming from the other direction turned and tried to get behind them, but the jeep cut them off. When they got to Cherry Avenue, they turned north up onto Signal Hill, and after a couple of turns, less than five minutes later they were pulling into the driveway of Richard and Char's hilltop home.

The four-car garage had plenty of room, and Richard hit a button to close the door behind them. As Andy and Abby got their kids out, Richie tugged on his Dad's sleeve. "Dad, can Meghan and I watch cartoons with Toby and Joey?"

Richard smiled. "Sure!" He winked at Abby.

She took her cue. "Take Joey by the hand into the theater, Richie. Then you turn things on, okay?"

"'Okay!" They went towards the other end of the house.

Char walked into their living room. "Let's sit down and relax. I want to know what happened down there! Abby, your suitcases won't be here for probably fifteen minutes or so."

"Our suitcases?!"

"Right! You heard Richard tell security that you and Andy will need full provisions. At this moment, officers from the Navy base, a man and a woman, are packing clothing for you, Andy, and the kids. Standing orders are to pack seasonal clothing for a month. They're good at it. When they get here, they'll carry your bags upstairs, and you and I can help them unpack your stuff into the guest room dressers and closet. Security already brought our kids here to the house."

Abby shook her head in amazement. "Incredible!"

Richard laughed as he and Andy sat down. "It's similar to concierge service in a first-class hotel. Char and I were initially exposed to this kind of service when we went on our honeymoon."

Andy's cell phone rang. He looked at the display, and it was Trina. "Hi Mom."

"Hi Andy. I just got a strange call from Malcolm Everly from the Press–Telegram. He wanted to be sure that you are going to be here so he could bring a camera crew. What's going on?"

"Abby and I got called to the hospital because the President had been shot, but was out of surgery. The First Lady was there. Abby and I prayed over him, and he woke up coughing. Dr. Cochran asked us to leave while he examined his patient, and we escaped with the Donovans. We're going to hide out at their home for a while."

There was a pause. "Andy. Stay there. Don't come tomorrow. I'll do the interview on my own. Tonight I'll warn your brother, your sister, and our pastor. I can confide in him about what has happened."

"Okay. Mom, don't try to visit here without calling first. The security around here is our government's best."

Trina laughed. "Good! I'll see you and Abby soon!"

"Bye." The connection ended.

Abby looked at him. "I take it you are not going to

join her for that interview tomorrow morning."

He chuckled. "You've got that right."

The house phone rang, and Char went to pick it up in the kitchen, but then she changed her mind and sprinted for the phone in the entry hall. Out of breath, she picked up the receiver. "Hello?"

"Hello, Char."

"Hello, General. I would imagine you want to know what happened."

"I've got a pretty good idea. Your friends prayed for the President. Joe Bahnmiller of the Secret Service called me and wanted them to come back because the President and First Lady want to thank them. I explained how, for security reasons, and to avoid the media, the four of you had to leave. I suspect that all of you will be invited to the White House soon."

Char laughed. "That won't be new for Richard and me, but it will be for them."

"Yeah. In case you're wondering, all the media are now focused upon the attempted assassination. The President went out in a wheel chair into the Emergency Room waiting area, and there he met with a few journalists to assure them that the rumor that he had died was false. He'll spend the night in the hospital and go back to Washington tomorrow afternoon. The shooter was a terrorist, and he was part of a larger plot, which we are continuing to unravel. I'll be in touch." The connection ended.

Char turned and went back into the living room to join her friends. Before she could sit down, the doorbell rang, and she went to the door.

"Good afternoon, Mrs. Donovan." A tall lieutenant smiled at her. "We have a larger crew than you perhaps expected. We packed the entire family and included the toys."

Richard, Andy, and Abby approached the door. Char turned to them. "They've packed up all your clothing and toys." She turned. "Lieutenant, did you bring their crib and playpen?"

He grinned. "Absolutely, Ma'am. We aim to please!"

While the children continued to watch cartoons in the theater, four civilians, two sailors, and two waves arranged furniture, clothing, and toys upstairs. It took less than a half hour.

They thanked the sailors and waves, and Char tipped them. Then they sat down in the living room, exhausted. Char looked at her watch. "Abby, I'll welcome help this time for dinner. Bible study neighbors will be here in less than an hour." They stood up. "There's plenty of food, but we've got to get it ready."

Abby nodded as they walked towards the kitchen. "Why not plan dinner for after Bible study, like we've done a couple of times during the summer. While you start dinner, I'll fix the kids some snacks to hold them over."

"Great!"

+ + +

Before Bible study began, all were talking about the attempted assassination. Jim and Rita, living across the street, were curious about both SUVs being in the garage. Rita was subtly excited. "Were the four of you there when President Riley came in?"

Richard shook his head. "President Riley and the First Lady came in an ambulance. While the President was being checked in and examined, the First Lady, knowing that we live here on Signal Hill, called us."

Char nodded. "We arrived just as the President was being brought back to the emergency ward because intensive care was full. I suggested that we get Andy and Abby there to join us for prayer, and the Secret Service arranged it."

Jim raised his eyebrows. "So all four of you got to see the President?"

Andy nodded. "Abby and I were there only briefly. We prayed together while Char was keeping the kids in the SUV. When it looked like the President was going to be all right, the three of us left, Char picked us up, and we came up here."

Abby smiled. "It was a real privilege to pray for the president with the First Lady!"

Jim looked at Andy. "How soon will the new parking lot be opened for use?"

Andy looked up briefly. "I hope it will open next month, but the way things are going, we'll continue to be using the shuttles for another couple of months."

Abby nodded. "Andy gets fewer complaints about the parking situation because everyone remembers the concert and knows that we're working on the problem."

12.
God Does Everything Well

The media furor died down after two weeks, and Andy and Abby moved back home. For months, the President and First Lady tried to set up a time for the four of them to visit Washington. During the Spring and Summer, however, Richard and Char's concert schedule was very busy. Finally, Bobbi Zealand set up a September concert for Richard in Philadelphia. It brought back wonderful memories to be there at the Kimmel Center with the Philadelphia Orchestra's conductor, who was also a friend. Richard played the Grieg Piano Concerto with them, which brought back lots of fine memories. For an encore he did Debussy's *L'isle Joyeuse.*

After Richard did a Sunday matinee, he flew with Char and the Hickmans to Washington. Since the private dinner at the White House was not until eight, they checked into the Sofitel Hotel. They walked towards the elevators.

"Andy! Andy Hickman!" The voice came from the other side of the hotel lobby. A blonde woman waved and walked over to them. "I'm sure you don't remember me, but I will never forget you, and I keep you in my prayers."

Andy smiled. "Thank you for your prayer support. Where did we meet?"

"After you scattered your father's ashes at sea, later that evening you were on the bow of the ship by yourself, and I approached you. We talked, and then you prayed for me."

Andy was thoughtful. "If I remember correctly, your name is Kristal. Isn't that correct?"

"Yes! You remember! I was taking that cruise as a final fling. I had terminal cancer and was not supposed to live more than a month or two at most. You put your hand on my head and silently prayed for me."

Andy smiled. "I remember! Praise God, you appear to be in pretty good health."

Richard, Char, and Abby gathered around closer.

"It's more than pretty good! The week after the cruise I saw my doctor, and I have been cancer-free for five years now!"

All of them were smiling and saying, "Praise God!"

"This is my wife, Abby, and our friends, Char and Richard Donovan."

Kristal shook hands with them. "You two are the musicians! It is so nice to meet you!"

Kristal gave Andy a hug and then stepped back. "Thank you again!" Andy nodded. She looked at her watch. "Oh, my! The shuttle will pick me up in just a moment. "I'm so glad I've gotten to meet you, — and to see you again, Andy - at least briefly. God bless you all!"

They all smiled as she quickly turned, went to get her suitcase, and got on the shuttle.

Andy gazed at his wife and his friends with a smile. "All that God does, God does well!"

<u>Other books by the author available at Amazon.com:</u>

<u>Gaardian Tales (Christian Fantasy Fiction)</u>
Life Before Conception
Starlight Adventures
The Still Small Voice
Stepping Beyond
The Gaardian Saga [The four above in one volume]

<u>Other Christian Fiction</u>
Casting Lots
Tom's Town

<u>Poetry and Inspiration</u>
Faith and Yosemite [Christian poetry with pictures]
Faith Fuel
Lasting Love
Walking in Faith
Seed Thoughts for Christian Prayer and Meditation

<u>Yosemite Picture Books</u>
Ever-Changing Yosemite Valley
Faith and Yosemite [see above]
Portraits of El Capitan
Portraits of Half Dome
Starlight Over Yosemite
Yosemite Textures and Shadows